SIREN'S STORM

SIREN'S STORM

Lisa Papademetriou

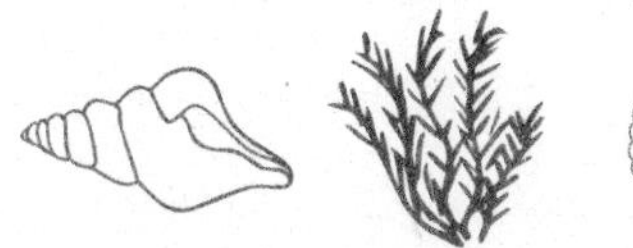

Alfred A. Knopf
New York

THIS IS A BORZOI BOOK PUBLISHED BY ALFRED A. KNOPF

Visit us on the Web! www.randomhouse.com/teens

Educators and librarians, for a variety of teaching tools, visit us at www.randomhouse.com/teachers

Library of Congress Cataloging-in-Publication Data
Papademetriou, Lisa.
Siren's storm / Lisa Papademetriou. — 1st ed.
p. cm.
ISBN 978-0-375-84245-0 (trade) — ISBN 978-0-375-94245-7 (lib. bdg.) — ISBN 978-0-375-89778-8 (ebook)
[1. Supernatural—Fiction. 2. Seaside resorts—Fiction. 3. Sirens (Mythology)—Fiction. 4. Calypso (Greek mythology)—Fiction. 5. Long Island (N.Y.)—Fiction.]
I. Title.
PZ7.P1954Shr 2011
[Fic]—dc22
2010029106

The text of this book is set in 11-point Bookman Light.

Printed in the United States of America
July 2011
10 9 8 7 6 5 4 3 2 1

First Edition

For George

Chapter One

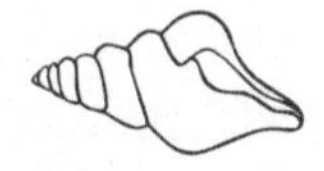

From the Walfang Gazette
Walfang Braces for Storm

Tropical Storm Bonita—packing winds up to 50 miles per hour and waves of up to 20 feet—is scheduled to reach Walfang by 3:00 Wednesday afternoon. Residents in some areas have been urged to evacuate, but many refuse to leave. "We're Long Islanders," said Harry Russell, owner of Russell Feed and Hardware. "You can't expect a little rain to frighten us."

But Bonita will likely be much worse than a little rain. "Although Bonita has not been classified a hurricane, it will definitely cause damage on the island. Just because it isn't as bad as the 1938 hurricane doesn't mean it isn't serious," declared Dr. Phyllis Ovid. The 1938 storm, the "Long Island Express," left 700 dead and 63,000 homeless, and is commonly considered one of the worst natural disasters in U.S. history. Although Bonita will not pack an equal punch, Dr. Ovid said, "people should be prepared for power loss, perhaps lasting several days."

Indeed, residents do seem to be hunkering down. "Our shelves are empty," claimed Sheila Danbury, owner of the

> Pick and Drive on King Road. "I think we've got five cans of soup left."
>
> Federal safety experts recommend that residents reinforce windows, fill the bathtub with water, and . . .

Will nosed the truck forward, picking his way along the slick street. Fat raindrops thrummed like heavy fingers against the faded orange hood, while water swirled around the tires, rushing toward drains already clogged with debris. The windshield wipers beat their *squeak, thunk, squeak, thunk* against the rippled water that sluiced down the glass. Will squinted to see the black ribbon that stretched out before him. It was ten o'clock in the morning, and the rain was steadily getting worse. He turned the knob on the radio, but all he got was static. *I'm lucky the wheels work,* Will thought. His uncle's truck was an old tank. Solid as a boulder, and just as high-tech. The boat hitch rattled over the road, dragging behind the truck like a lame leg.

The streets were empty, but Will stopped at the red light anyway. He was a careful driver, which had always amused his older brother, Tim. "Nobody cares if you go over the speed limit by five miles per hour," Tim had always said. "Come on, put the pedal to the metal, bro!" But Tim wasn't with him this morning, so Will could be as careful as he liked. He didn't want to get into an accident on the way to pick up the boat.

The light changed, and Will moved forward, but a moment later he slammed on the brakes. A sheet of corrugated metal—an escaped piece of roofing from someone's shed—thwacked against the side of the truck, momentarily blocking the driver's-side window.

"Jesus," Will whispered, his heart hammering. Then the wind shifted and the metal flipped up, flew over the hood of the truck, and sailed down the street. Will watched as it tumbled and finally fell, sliding under the front steps of City Hall.

With a sigh, Will gently pressed the accelerator.

"Shit!" he shouted as a figure darted in front of the truck. Will's right leg cramped as he ground his foot against the brake pedal. A thud sent a wave of nausea through him, and it took a moment for him to realize that he hadn't hit the figure—it had hit *him.* Bright green eyes stared up at him through the windshield. The girl's palms were flat against the hood of the truck, almost as if she were holding it in place.

Sudden music blasted from the radio, and Will startled so badly that he nearly hit his head against the roof. He felt sick. Green cat eyes, long black hair—that was all he was aware of. That and the thought, *She's alive. She's okay. She's alive. You didn't.* Still, his hands were shaking. A flood of fear surged through him, and then, right on its heels, rage.

I could have killed her! He was furious about it—about the idea that she might have made him responsible for something like that.

"Are you okay?" Will shouted, although he knew his voice must have been muffled through the glass.

The girl looked at him a moment longer, then turned and darted off. She disappeared between two nearby buildings. *Almost like the sheet of metal slipping beneath the steps,* Will thought. *Like a knife disappearing into wood.*

Will took a deep breath, then another. His head was light. Finally he became aware that he was sitting in the middle of an intersection. He didn't want to move, but he didn't have much of a choice. Tentatively he pressed the accelerator. The truck inched forward.

Will tapped his fingers against the steering wheel, trying to keep his mind on the road. But he couldn't stop thinking about that girl and her strange green eyes. Her skin was pale and smooth, like the inside of a shell. Will felt a flash of confusion. She seemed to be about his age—seventeen—and looked familiar. Then again, this was a pretty small town. Everyone looked familiar. *Do I know her?* Will wondered.

But this girl was beautiful. Beautiful in a way he wouldn't have forgotten—not even with his questionable memory. Besides, it was summer. Walfang was a tourist town, and the population surged during the months of June, July, and August. *Maybe she's a summer person. . . .*

After three blocks, Will could see the ocean. The dock where he kept the Bermuda-rigged sailing dinghy was close to the end of town, at the rocky spit that jutted into the sea. Most of the Hamptons were white sand over rolling dunes, but Walfang was at the far tip of Long Island and had dark granite parts that felt almost New Englandy. The dock housed several small craft and was partially protected by a cove. But with a storm like this headed straight for Walfang, the cove would offer as much protection as an umbrella in a cyclone.

Even now, waves beat the beach, exploding against the rocks that lined the coast. Foam spewed into the air, meeting the rain as it fell. *Water on water,* Will thought as he parked at the edge of the docks.

"If you'd drive more than five miles per hour, I wouldn't have to wait for you." The big bear of a man grinned as Will stepped onto the pitching sailboat.

"Sorry, Uncle Carl."

But Carl wrapped one arm around Will and gave him a playful slap on the back. "I've been here a full ten minutes!" He let out a full laugh that threatened to blow back the hurricane winds. "Nothing but a little rain so far," Carl said. "But the weathermen say it's likely to make landfall near Walfang, so we might as well get the *Vagabond* secured. I'll tie up the main lines."

The wind lashed at Will's face as he made for the sails. Nearby, boats rocked on the swelling waves. Will's father had thought the *Vagabond* could ride out the storm if Will took down the sails. But Will didn't want to risk it, not with his brother's boat. Luckily, his uncle Carl had understood completely.

The sky met the sea in shades of deep gray, and white-tipped waves roared toward the shore. They hurled themselves against the beach in growing fury before hissing backward in retreat. The fat white gulls that usually wheeled over the docks in greedy anticipation had taken shelter under the eaves of the nearby snack bar. They watched the sky warily as rain pelted the wooden shack. Their silence was almost eerie. There was no sound but the ocean and the uneven creak and knock of the bobbing boats.

Will scanned the empty beach. Everything was a shade darker than usual. Thick clouds blotted out the sun, and the rain had turned the rocks black and the sand to a shade of caramel. It was as if darkness had already fallen. He noticed that his uncle had stopped moving. Carl was staring out to sea, a strange look on his face. "Everything okay?" Will asked.

Carl turned to him. "Do you hear that?"

Will shook his head and indicated his right ear. He'd lost his hearing on that side the summer before. "What is it?"

Carl shrugged. "I don't know. I thought I heard—" He shrugged. "Sounded like music."

"Good for dancing?" Will teased, and Carl laughed.

"Good for sleeping, more like," his uncle said. "Eh, it's gone now."

"Probably just a creaky boat," Will said.

"Yeah," Carl agreed, although he didn't look convinced.

Will turned back to his work. He touched the mainmast with a light finger. The sail had gone up in flames last summer, leaving a dark scar on the boat. It was lucky that the whole *Vagabond* hadn't burned—it had tipped, dousing the fire and saving itself.

Will secured the sail and pulled a cover over it, snapping it securely into place. Taking a deep breath, he looked up at the rocks on the shore.

Will grasped the handrail as if the boat had lurched beneath him. A sudden nausea rose in his throat.

One of the black rocks had *moved.*

The rock was still for a moment, then moved again, and with heart-stopping clarity Will realized that a human figure was picking its way—headfirst—down the steep escarpment. The figure had long, delicate limbs that moved with surprising speed across the rocks, almost like a spider. Will hurried to the canvas storage bag and sorted through his brother's collection of junk to pull out a pair of binoculars. He trained them on the figure. Just as he'd thought—it was the girl from this morning. He was almost sure of it. She had the same long black hair, the same dark olive windbreaker.

What's she doing? Will wondered as he watched her pause briefly at the bottom. She faced the sea, then began to walk toward it.

Salt stung Will's face as the frigid water reached her ankles.

"Wait!" Will shouted. "Wait!"

But she didn't pause or even glance toward him as she waded into the water. Will hopped over the rail and raced down the dock, but the water was already up to her waist.

"Stop!"

She turned and looked at him. Her face was awash with confusion, and he thought she would turn back. But she didn't move. The wind tore the scream from his throat as a wave crashed over her, swallowing her whole. "No!"

Her head did not bob back to the surface as Will raced to the water's edge. "Wait!" Icy claws tore at his shins as he waded into the water. "No!"

For a moment he thought he saw the thick ropes of her hair. He reached out, but his hand drew back only seaweed. Her head didn't reappear above the surface.

A wave loomed before him like sheer wall. Will tried to dive into the calmer base of the wave, but it blasted against him like dynamite, knocking him down. For a sickening moment his feet couldn't find purchase. In the tumble, he'd lost his sense of how to become upright. Churning sand filled his eyes—he couldn't see. But his fear was lost in his need to find the girl. His arms reached out for her, but she wasn't there. He couldn't breathe. . . .

Suddenly he felt a strong hand on his arm, and a moment later his head broke through to the rainy surface. "Will!" Uncle Carl was there, pulling him toward shore. "Will—are you okay?"

Will tried to speak but sucked in salt water. He coughed violently.

The waves took no pity, continuing their relentless assault. Will's mind was muddled, but his body held a deep survival instinct. Without thinking, he allowed his uncle to haul him toward shore. They ducked and let the waves pass over them until they were at the breakers. Carl did not let go of him, not even when the waves slithered only to their ankles and they collapsed to their knees on the sandy beach.

"What were you thinking?" Carl shouted as coughs racked Will's chest. "What the hell were you doing?"

Will shook his head. "I couldn't—" Another fit of coughing overtook him. The seawater that lined his mouth made him want to gag. But he had to say something. He had to let his uncle know that it wasn't his fault. "I couldn't reach her."

Something flickered in Carl's eyes—something that Will couldn't read. "Who?"

Rain lashed at Will's face; water streamed into his eyes. "The girl with black hair."

Carl shook his head. "What girl?"

"She was walking into the water. I tried to stop her." Will gestured to the crashing surf. "She was right there—five yards ahead of me."

Carl shook his head, but he didn't say anything else. Will felt his silence like a slap. "You'd better get on home," Carl said. His voice was calm, quiet. He stood up and yanked Will's hand, pulling him to his feet. "I'll finish up on the boat."

"I came out to help you," Will protested. His voice felt feeble as it rose from his throat, and was made even thinner in the wild air.

"You get on home," Carl repeated. "Take my car; I'll take the truck." He patted Will on the back with a hand like an anchor. "I'll be there soon." He looked deeply into Will's eyes for a moment, then turned and started across the sand.

Will felt sick as he stared out at the coal-gray water that roared at him. *What happened?* A large wave crashed at the break point, then smoothed and reached toward him like an arm unfolding. It grabbed at his feet, then retreated and sank wearily into the sand. There was no sign of life beyond the breakers. The water held no trace of his struggle to save the girl, no record that she had ever been there at all.

Chapter Two

From "The Sailor's Song" (Traditional)

The waves doth rage
And the wind doth blow
But a brave young man was he,
For he'd heard a voice
Singing on the storm
So he went down to the sea . . .

There was water all around her. She couldn't see the horizon, and somehow she knew the shore was a long way off. She wasn't sure how she'd gotten here.

The moon shone down on the calm black water. The stars were out—more stars than she had ever seen before, like a blanket of diamonds. And the constellations were strange. She wondered where she was.

Farther in, her mind whispered. *Farther in.*

She swam forward, then stopped, treading water. Something brushed her arm, and she drew it away quickly. The movement caused a splash that sounded deafening in the silence of the dark sea.

She became aware that the edge of the horizon had shifted slightly. A black shape had blotted out part of the stars—a mountain. She swam toward it, wondering how she could have missed noticing it before.

She concentrated on swimming, but her arms were tired. She looked up, expecting to feel despair at the mountain's distance. But, surprisingly, it seemed much closer now. She was making progress.

She redoubled her efforts, moving with great effort through the sea. The next time she looked up, she realized that the mountain was almost on top of her.

But it was no mountain.

She struggled against the water in a desperate attempt to swim backward, but it was useless. The wave slammed against her. She was caught in the giant wall of water. Claws scraped at her face, her legs. The tsunami had churned up so much debris that driftwood and pieces of shell scratched and bit at her like living things.

Her lungs strained.

I have to swim toward the surface, she thought. But there was another voice in her mind. *Down,* it whispered, *down.*

And then she saw the eyes. They gleamed through the dark water like silver coins at the bottom of a pool. Then—teeth. They revealed themselves slowly in a dangerous, razor-like grin. "Gretchen," the thing said.

Gretchen tried to cry out, but her mouth filled with water.

An arm reached toward her, grabbing her shoulder in a grip that burned like a brand. "Gretchen," the thing repeated. "Gretchen!"

"Gretchen!"

The voice changed, deepened.

"Gretchen!"

And suddenly a man stood before her. Wild hair, dark eyes, black goatee, a strange dark mark like a flower near his temple. Water streamed down his face like tears. "Gretchen!" he cried.

She pressed her palms against his chest. "Dad?" Gretchen looked around. She wasn't in the water. There were boards beneath her bare feet. She looked down at her dark blue T-shirt and plaid pajama bottoms. Her clothes were sticking to her limply. "I'm all wet."

"It's still raining," Johnny said as water lashed the porch. "The storm hasn't passed yet. Are you okay?" Creases appeared at the corners of his dark eyes. It was an expression Gretchen's father wore often lately—he looked worried.

"I'm fine." Gretchen glanced out over the front yard. It looked like the storm had already taken out one of the smaller weeping willows on the edge of the creek that ran through their property. Even in the darkness, Gretchen could see limbs littered across her front lawn. "Why am I on the porch?" she asked. "What time is it?"

"Midnight," Johnny said. Naturally, Gretchen's father was still wearing his jeans and faded concert T-shirt. He didn't go to bed before three in the morning most nights.

"I thought you were asleep," he said. Then, hesitating, "I mean—I guess you were."

"It's been five weeks," Gretchen said. Since the last sleepwalking incident, she meant. That was nearly a record.

"Why are we still standing out here?" Johnny took her elbow and guided her through the front door. "Do you want some cocoa, or something? It's chilly." He grabbed a cashmere throw from the faded couch and swept it over her shoulders. He touched her chin gently, then led the way toward the kitchen. Gretchen's cat, Bananas, took one look at her and skittered under the couch.

"Thanks for the support," Gretchen told the cat.

The house was warm and comfortable, but Gretchen kept the blanket around her shoulders. Her father liked to cluck and fuss over her, and she knew it made him happy to think that he was keeping her warm, even though Gretchen hardly ever felt cold. All winter long she would wander the streets of Manhattan with only a light jacket and no hat. It drove her father crazy. Even here, in the summer house, he kept jackets in the hallway and blankets on the couches. "Just in case," he said. Unlike her, Johnny was cold-blooded.

Gretchen sat down at the wooden table in the breakfast nook as her father walked to the cupboard. She looked around the cozy kitchen. *I could live here all year.* The thought was comforting . . . especially since it was starting to look like she'd have to.

Johnny stood staring at the cupboards. He looked baffled.

"Cold," Gretchen said.

"What? You're cold?"

"No—you are," Gretchen told him.

Johnny looked at her quizzically as he touched the lotus tattoo on his temple.

"Wrong cupboard," Gretchen explained. "Ice cold."

Johnny scooted to the right.

"Warmer," Gretchen told him.

He moved farther to the right.

"Warmer. Warmer. Getting hot."

Johnny opened the cupboard and rummaged around on the middle shelf until he found the cocoa. He leaned against the counter, studying the label. "But this is for baking," he said.

Gretchen sighed. "Let me do it."

"I can make cocoa," Johnny protested.

"Right." Gretchen rolled her eyes and shook the blanket from her shoulders. "Just like you can cook chicken."

"The fire department guy said they handled fires like that all the time," her father protested as she took the cocoa from his hand.

Johnny was pretty famous for his incompetence in the kitchen. The gourmet meals they'd enjoyed when Yvonne—Gretchen's mother—was behind the apron had devolved to boxes of mac and cheese and Chinese takeout in the years since she had moved out. But Gretchen didn't care. She had always hated fancy food.

"He was clearly a Johnny Ellis fan," Gretchen countered as she yanked open the fridge. "He was just being kind."

"Nobody's a Johnny Ellis fan," her dad corrected. "Studio musicians don't have fans."

"Oh, please." The milk hissed softly at the rim as

the pan heated up. "Everyone knows who you've recorded with. They're all hoping that we'll have a pool party one day and invite all of their favorite rock stars."

"Well . . ." Johnny stroked his goatee, pretending to think it over. "We'd have to get a pool . . . and I'd have to make some friends."

Gretchen let the sugar fall into the milk in a steady stream. Steam started to rise from the cocoa, and she poured it carefully into two mugs.

"What's that?" Johnny asked as she passed him a mug. His favorite—the one that said World's Best Dad.

Gretchen cocked her head. "Cocoa."

Johnny rolled his eyes. "Yeah—I got it," he said as he blew across the top of the steaming liquid. "I'm not a total idiot. I *meant,* what's that song you're humming?"

Gretchen sat still. She hadn't even realized she'd been humming. "I don't know," she said.

"Hum it again."

Gretchen tried, but the tune was like sand that slipped through her fingers. "I can't."

Johnny shrugged. "Too bad. Could've made me a million."

"Next time," Gretchen told him. But she wasn't even sure what she meant. *What next time?*

Will looked out his window as the raindrops splattered the glass. It was past midnight, but he couldn't fall asleep. His mind was whirling with thoughts and images. That girl—he couldn't get her green eyes out of his mind. When he closed his eyes, he saw them clearly—luminous, with hypnotic intensity.

Guernsey let out a soft snore from her place at the foot of Will's bed. Will stroked her gray-flecked black coat softly, so as not to wake her. *Let the old girl sleep,* he thought as the Labrador shifted slightly, dreaming.

Will's room was directly over the kitchen, and his father's and uncle's bass voices floated up to him. When he was a child, Will had always found their talk soothing. Tim had been interested in the parental gossip, but Will tried to listen not to the words but just to the calming drone of the voices, like the crash of the sea. It was hard now, though, since the words were about him.

"You should have seen him." Carl's voice was a sigh, and Will could picture his uncle sitting at the ancient wood table, swigging a bottle of non-alcoholic beer. Will's father always kept the fridge stocked with them in case Carl came over.

Carl had waited until Will's mother went to sleep to mention anything about the incident on the beach.

Carl is a wise man, Will thought. *Mom would've had to be strapped to something.*

"He looked . . . well, to be honest with you, Bert, he looked crazy."

Will's father let out a soft hissing sound. "It's the timing."

"Next week. I know." There was a gentle clink as Carl set his bottle on the table.

Next week. The God's honest truth was that Will

hadn't realized that it had been almost a year. But of course it had. *It's the end of June, isn't it?*

It was frightening how little he thought about the night his brother died. He used to think about it all the time, trying to remember what had happened. He would talk to anyone who would listen in an attempt to puzzle out the events of that night. Will knew that he and Tim had gone sailing at sunset. There was nothing unique about that. Except Tim hadn't come back. And Will had. The police had found him on the beach, unconscious. He'd been wet, his face covered in blood. Nobody knew how he'd gotten there. And nobody knew what had happened to Tim.

Eventually people stopped listening to Will. They would sit with him while he talked, sure, but their eyes would lose focus or drift to the clock on the wall. Will could tell that some of them didn't believe that his memory was like an empty shell. He had to remember something, they'd say. *Something.* But Will *didn't* remember.

Why did they find me when they never found Tim?

It was a question with no answer.

The wind howled mournfully through the trees. It was dark, but Will could see the branches bending with the gusts. He wondered how many trunks would be torn from the earth before the night was over.

"Don't say anything to Evelyn." His father again.

"Of course not. I just don't know—maybe there *was* a girl, Bert. But—"

"In this storm?" Will's father sounded doubtful.

"I didn't see anything."

"There was nothing to see." Silence. And then, "He'll be better in a couple of weeks. This anniversary is taking a toll."

"I know it is."

Will lay on his back, still feeling the motion of the waves with his body. He could still see that girl. He could see the water as it closed over her, gobbled her up. She had seemed so real.

He stood up and went to the bathroom. The fluorescent light flickered on, revealing his greenish face in the mirror. *Maybe I* am *crazy,* he thought, staring into his own eyes. No matter how often he saw it, he couldn't get used to the purplish scar that ran diagonally across his forehead and sliced down the top of his cheekbone. His sandy hair covered it most of the time. But sometimes the wind would push it back, and a passing stranger would stare. It made Will feel like Frankenstein—like someone stitched back together. Especially in a place like Walfang, where all of the summer people were surgically perfected.

It wouldn't be so bad if I could just remember, Will thought as he pulled open the medicine cabinet. *If I just knew what happened.*

Will pulled out an orange bottle and unscrewed the white plastic top. His doctor had prescribed sleeping pills, but Will hated taking them. They made him groggy and lethargic the next day.

Then again, so did staying awake all night.

He shook two pills into his palm and popped them into his mouth. Then he scooped cool water from the faucet to wash them down. He put the bottle back and closed the medicine chest, then clicked off the light.

Will settled back under the ancient quilt his great-aunt had stitched and listened to the wind's complaints. He tucked his feet under Guernsey's warm body. *There's a hurricane happening on the other side of this wall,* Will thought.

The wind picked up. The sturdy oak near the farm stand stood tall, refusing to bend, but the wind simply redoubled in rage. A crack like a gunshot, then several pops and a groan as the wind delivered its vengeance. The oak leaned, then toppled with an explosion and a strange silver tinkle.

"Greenhouse," Will's father said.

Footsteps, and the sound of the kitchen door opening and slamming shut. The house was suddenly silent. Will lay perfectly still in the darkness.

A year ago, Will's father would have shouted up at both of his sons to get their asses downstairs and help. But not now.

Will curled onto his side, like a question mark. He knew he'd fall asleep eventually. He just had to wait.

Chapter Three

From the Walfang Gazette
City Cleanup Scheduled Today

Walfang's mayor, Claire Hutchinson, has asked all city employees to assist with the cleanup of city beaches today. Tropical Storm Bonita didn't cause as much damage as forecasted or feared, but it still packed high winds and waves that have left the beaches riddled with detritus.

"Our economy depends on the tourist trade," Mayor Hutchinson read from a prepared statement last night at a press conference. "When tourists come to Walfang, they expect to see the pristine white sand beaches we're famous for." A spokesman for the Department of Public Works . . .

"Good morning, sunshine!" Gretchen chirped as Will shuffled groggily into the kitchen the next morning. She slid two fried eggs onto a plate and headed to rescue the toast from the toaster. Will's dad had been meaning to fix the pop-up feature for the past eight years, but Gretchen knew its quirks.

"What are you doing here?" Will asked, blinking at her with heavy lids. "Why does it smell like bacon?"

"Because I made you breakfast," Gretchen replied as she set the plate before him. "I figured bacon would probably be the only thing that could wake you up."

Will glanced at the clock: eleven-thirty. And here he was, in his own kitchen, while the girl from next door was cooking away like Snow White bent on feeding an army of mining dwarves. That was so Gretchen. She only spent summers in Walfang, but whenever she and her father appeared, they just picked up as if they had never left. "Where is everybody?"

"I think your dad's at the hardware store. Your mom is—"

"Well, look who finally rolled out of bed," Evelyn Archer said as she walked in from the living room. Her dark eyes scowled at Will. "Your father could use your help, you know. Humberto can't come in today."

Will scooped up a forkful of egg. Arguing with his mother never got him anywhere.

"Bert isn't here right now," Gretchen told her.

Mrs. Archer removed her laser glance from Will's face and turned to Gretchen. "I didn't know you were in town."

"Here I am!" Gretchen singsonged. She paced over to the coffeepot and poured the dark, rich liquid into Will's mother's favorite cup. "He told me he had to get the tractor fixed in town—said he'd be back in a couple of hours." She held out the mug, and Mrs. Archer accepted it gratefully.

"Ah," she said as she pulled a long whiff of the coffee. "It never tastes this good when I make it." She sat down heavily in the wooden chair. The caning sighed under her weight. Will's mother still had the high cheekbones and fine features that had made her a famous local beauty in her youth. But she had turned matronly, especially in the past year. She no longer bothered to highlight her hair, which was now cut short in a utilitarian style. And she wore mostly shorts and baggy shirts in neutral colors. It was as if she were trying to turn herself invisible.

Gretchen wiggled her eyebrows at Will, who was silently chewing the last of his bacon.

"What did you do to your face?" Mrs. Archer asked.

"My face?" Gretchen's fingers flew to her cheeks.

"She means your nose ring," Will translated.

"You haven't seen this yet?" Gretchen tossed her long blond hair and angled her face so that Will's mother could get a better view of the tiny sapphire that glittered at the impression on her right nostril. "I got it while we were in India in January. It's very traditional there." Gretchen grinned playfully and poked Mrs. Archer in the arm. "You should get one, Evelyn. Or maybe an eyebrow ring—they're very in right now."

Mrs. Archer snorted a laugh and rolled her eyes.

"You'd be the talk of the town," Gretchen teased.

"I'm already the talk of the town," Mrs. Archer snapped, and took another long slug of her coffee.

An awkward silence pulsed through the room.

"Well," Will said as he wiped up the last of the egg with a crust of toast, "this has been great, but I think I should—"

"Will's heading into town with me," Gretchen

announced as she slapped the back of his chair with a kitchen towel. "I need to pick up a few things. Okay, Evelyn?"

Will's mother just shrugged a reply. "Ask your father why we never see him anymore."

"He sends his regards," Gretchen called. She was already pulling Will out the door.

"You drove here?" Will asked when he saw her car in the driveway.

"I knew we were going out, and I'm not riding on the back of your bike, thanks."

"You knew we were going out?"

"I want ice cream, and you're coming with me."

"Why didn't you just eat breakfast?"

"I *did* eat breakfast. At eight, like a normal person. Now it's time for ice cream." Gretchen yanked him toward the battered orange Gremlin she bombed around in. The thing looked like an antique, and handled like one. She referred to it as her "pothole detector," since it always managed to find every single one on the road.

"You're lucky my mother likes you," Will said dryly as Gretchen sent gravel flying.

"I'm the kooky daughter she never wanted," Gretchen said.

Will laughed. "Yeah, and I'm the non-kooky son she never liked."

Gretchen winced. "That's not true."

Will shrugged. He looked out the window. "So I can be kooky sometimes."

Gretchen punched him playfully. "Shut up." She

drove slowly, picking her way around fallen branches. "Dad says Route 27 is clear."

"Won't have a problem merging onto it today."

"Let's hope." Gretchen turned at the fork, and suddenly the main road came into view. The two-lane highway was usually clogged to a crawl with summer people, but not this morning. *I guess everyone's busy yelling at their gardeners to get the fallen branches out of the hedges,* Will thought as Gretchen turned onto the road. In a moment they were flying. Gretchen's car didn't have air-conditioning, not that you ever really needed it in Walfang. The ocean air was always cool, and it smelled sweet—like cut grass. The summer people had planted immaculate gardens between the acres still used by horse breeders and potato farmers.

"When did you get back?" Will asked.

"Thursday."

"Today is Thursday."

"Last Thursday."

Will turned his face away from hers. He stared out the window in silence. He wasn't surprised, of course. He'd noticed the lights were on at night. He'd seen Johnny's car in the driveway.

Last year Gretchen hadn't even stopped at her own house before coming over to the Archers'. Johnny's vintage silver Mercedes pulled into the Archer driveway and Gretchen spilled out, shouting and whooping at the top of her lungs. Tim was working at the stand, and Gretchen tackled him first, wrapping him in a huge hug. Then she'd found Will in the tomato house and insisted that they go to the beach—even though she never swam in the ocean, Gretchen loved the sand—at four o'clock sharp. So they had. But that had been last year.

Gretchen pulled off the highway onto a shady lane lined with houses that were large, but tastefully so.

"So, after ten months, you just decided to come over and make me some breakfast?"

Gretchen was silent. Will looked out the window, letting the breeze blow through his hair. His father liked to tease him. "Get a haircut," he'd say. But Will liked the long hair. He let it hang, curtain-like, over his scar.

Tim had always buzzed his hair off at the beginning of the summer. By summer's end, he'd looked scruffy again. Will had preferred the scruffy version of his brother—half-grown beard, shorts two sizes too big. With his chiseled jaw and long, aquiline nose, Tim's good looks could be intimidating. At the beginning of the summer, Tim always looked like someone who could pull you over and give you a speeding ticket or slap cuffs on you. By the end of the summer, with his hair grown out again, he looked like a vacationing movie star.

Will glanced over at Gretchen. One hand was on the steering wheel, the other hanging out the window. Her posture was carefree, but her face was serious—lost in thought. Will noticed how pale she was. She had dark circles under her eyes.

"How are you sleeping?" Will asked.

"Eh—I got out last night."

"That could be dangerous, you know," Will told her.

She sighed, and the sparkle in her voice seemed to drain away. "I know."

Will wondered how she had the energy to even pretend to be happy. He certainly didn't. It was all he could do to get out of bed, work at the stand, and exchange a few words with other human beings. Even brushing his teeth felt like a superhuman effort.

As they turned into the center of town, Will became aware that he was scanning the sidewalks for signs of the girl he'd seen yesterday. But the streets were mostly empty. He fought the urge to ask Gretchen if she'd ever seen anyone matching the girl's description. He didn't feel like explaining what had happened the day before. *Let it go,* he told himself.

Finally they pulled up in front of Sixteen Flavors. "I don't think I've ever heard you hum before," Will said as the car rattled to a stop.

Gretchen paused, her hand partway to the door handle. "I was humming?"

"Yeah."

She cocked her head. "How did it go?"

Will gave her a look. "You know that line of questioning will get you nowhere," he said. Will was completely tone-deaf.

The bell over the door jingled as Will and Gretchen stepped into the cool air of the ice cream shop. Sixteen Flavors served lunch, too, and the place was already filling up with locals and summer people looking for a bite in one of the few places in town that were open. Will said a little prayer of thanks that the girl smiling at them behind the counter was Rachel Finnegan. She was sweet and didn't talk much. She was also just a freshman, which meant she wasn't likely to dare to chat with them.

"Two scoops of peppermint stick on a sugar cone," Will said as he perched on the red stool.

"And can I get you anything?" Rachel asked Gretchen.

"No, that's for her," Will explained. "She always gets the same thing. I'll have a Coke."

Rachel turned to Gretchen with lifted eyebrows, and Gretchen nodded. Then Rachel looked at Will again, and her cheeks blushed pink. She looked down at the counter when she handed Will his Coke.

"Thanks, Rachel," he said, and she flushed even harder before she scurried to scoop out the ice cream.

Rachel handed Gretchen the ice cream cone, and Will waved off Gretchen's attempt to pay. "You buy the next one," he said.

Will held the door as Gretchen stepped into the sunshine. She nodded her thanks—she was busy licking an escaping drip from her ice cream.

Three guys with sleek, tanned chests and low-slung shorts were fixing a broken awning in front of a new restaurant, Paz. *Yay. Another pretentious restaurant.* When he was a kid, the streets had been lined with cute little stores that were run by people from Walfang. There had been Penny's Candy, Toys and More, Fitzgerald's—which everyone had always called the dime store—and the "nice" restaurant, Delia Mater's. All of those were gone now, except for Delia's, which had been renovated beyond recognition by a couple of New York City investors. Now, boutique after boutique lined the streets. Most of them offered impossible-to-wear fashions at the kind of prices usually reserved for major appliances.

A scrawny kid with lank black hair watched the workers from a stoop. When he saw Gretchen, he turned his huge dark eyes to her face and stared. He was gawking, really, with a gaze that didn't waver or blink. Will could tell the look made Gretchen uncomfortable, because she stiffened beside him. Will knew the kid. He wanted to tell Gretchen not to worry, that he was just a harmless dude who was a little crazy, but before Will could speak, she turned and asked, "Does that happen to you a lot?" She elbowed him in the ribs. "People just staring at you?"

Will gave her a wry smile. "What can I say? It ain't easy being this sexy. Seriously, that's just a sophomore kid—Kirk Worstler."

Gretchen chuckled, her limbs loosening a little, and she let Will steer her across the street, away from the skinny kid's piercing gaze. She seemed happy again, intent on her ice cream. Will was just starting to relax when Gretchen stopped suddenly and stood staring at a telephone pole. A vibrant green flyer blared that a local band—Minutia's Cousin—would be playing at the Old Barn on Saturday night. Gretchen reached out and touched the paper as if it were an old relic or a fragment from a dream.

Will read the flyer over Gretchen's shoulder. "Life goes on, I guess," he said.

Gretchen's eyes glowed, like paper that had

caught fire. "I can't believe they'd just—" She shook her head.

Will placed a gentle hand on her shoulder. He'd seen the flyers before, so it wasn't such a shock that Tim's band had somehow managed to go on without him. But Gretchen tensed, her fingers knotted into a tight fist. "Tim started that band," she said. "That was *Tim's* band."

Will shrugged. He could practically hear Alan and Rob and Ginny saying, "Tim would have wanted it this way." He was sure the band had gotten together and decided that keeping the name would be a tribute to their friend and the fulfillment of his wishes. Will thought it was interesting that everyone seemed to know what Tim would have wanted. He, personally, had no idea.

Will remembered the last time he and Gretchen had gone to hear Tim play. It had been an open-air concert on the lush green lawn in front of First Church. Minutia's Cousin played a strange fusion of classical and rock. Tim played classical guitar, Alan played flute and piccolo, Rob played percussion, and Ginny played the electric guitar and sang. Tim had arranged most of their music, stealing phrases and snippets from classical and updating the melodies. They were just starting to become well known locally—even now, their Facebook fans were a strange mix of teens and grayhairs. Gretchen had *loved* their music. She insisted that Will accompany her to every single concert, and she sometimes even sat in on rehearsals. Will had liked Minutia's Cousin, too—but mostly because it was Tim's band. Personally, Will preferred hip-hop, and he liked it loud. Minutia's Cousin sometimes sounded like glorified elevator music to him, but then again, he didn't know much about music.

Gretchen stood for a moment with her head bowed like the curve of a candlewick. Finally she seemed to pull herself together. She straightened up and frowned at the gaudy flyer. "They'll suck without him," she said lightly. She let Will's hand drop from her shoulder as she stepped away and tossed her ice cream cone into a garbage can.

Will could tell from the way she said it that he'd never see her at another Minutia's Cousin concert again. She'd always been friendly with Alan and Ginny—not Rob so much, because he hardly ever spoke—but if she saw them in the street now, she probably wouldn't even wave. That's how she was.

Gretchen liked to pretend that nothing bothered her. But Will knew better. Almost *everything* bothered her. More than once, she had confronted Will about something insensitive he'd said weeks earlier, words that had created tiny wounds that refused to heal. Even worse was when Gretchen would obsess over some slight she feared that she had caused Will. She would return days, sometimes weeks later with an overwrought apology for something that Will couldn't even recall. He didn't understand the way her mind worked. Things that meant nothing to him meant everything to her. But that was also why she fell into raptures at the sight of a flower or burst into tears while reading a poster for a stray dog. She was like something flammable, and everything was fuel for her fire.

Gretchen flipped her blond hair and slipped her arm through Will's. He put a warm hand on her bicep, but he didn't look at her. They fell into step down the quiet street. Most of the stores weren't open, but a few—like the hardware store—were humming with activity.

"That was a really good breakfast, by the way," Will said at last. "Thanks."

"You're welcome."

They walked a little farther. The town had recently refurbished the business district, and the pavement was set with red bricks. A few branches were down here and there, but it looked as if the city had cleaned everything up early in the morning.

Will stopped suddenly, his arm dropping from Gretchen's shoulder. Something in the window of an antiques store had caught his eye.

"What's up?" Gretchen asked.

He was looking at what seemed to be an ancient flute. A very familiar-looking flute. But he didn't want to have to try to explain it to Gretchen. Especially since he didn't know what he was explaining. Instead he just shook his head. "Nothing."

"Nothing? Nothing, like—nothing? Or nothing, like—dramatic pause—*nothing* that's really fraught with something?"

Will blinked at her. "Nothing, as in that's a cool flute. But the store isn't open, anyway, so forget it."

"Okay, keep your secrets." She pointed to the Help Wanted sign in the window of the vintage silver diner next door. "Destiny has led me here," she announced dramatically.

Will looked dubious. "You're going to work at Bella's? You'd get better tips at the Villa. Or that new Paz place."

Gretchen studied the caboose-style diner. The windows were filled with hand-lettered signs advertising specials—$2.99 for eggs, toast, bacon, coffee. Free ice cream with kids' meal. Breakfast served all day. It was located at the scruffy end of a nice street, next to a run-down liquor store. This corner was the only blot on the pristine block. And Bella's was the only place where the locals could still afford a meal. Most of the summer people never set foot in there.

"Rich people are crappy tippers," Gretchen replied. "How do I look?" She straightened the pale blue halter she was wearing with a pair of white denim shorts. "Do you think I should go home and change?"

"You look great," Will said. "You don't need to wear a business suit to get a waitressing job."

"Said like someone who works on a farm." Gretchen raked her fingers through her thick, wild blond hair and smeared on some lip balm. She peeked at herself in the reflection of the glass and took a deep breath. "Wish me luck," she said to Will.

Will studied her a moment. "Why are you even doing this? You've got plenty of money."

Gretchen looked pensive, as if she was about to

say something heavy. Then she seemed to change her mind, and flashed him a smile. "What else am I supposed to do all day?" she asked. "Sit around on the beach and work on my tan?"

Will shrugged. "That's what most girls do."

Gretchen put a hand on her hip. "I'm not most girls," she told him.

Will gave her a brotherly arm punch. "Yeah," he said. "I noticed."

The chain saw screamed as Mr. Archer sliced into the fallen tree's thick trunk. As he approached his house from the rear—cutting across Gretchen's yard to get to his own—Will got a good look at the greenhouse wreckage. It wasn't as bad as he'd feared. The oak had glanced off the sloped roof, popping some windows and crushing a few tender seedlings. Two feet over, and the greenhouse would have been totaled. The tree lay like a fallen giant on the side near the house. The roots were still attached at the base, and it had left a huge hole in the earth.

Will strode toward his father, who was cutting the trunk into eighteen-inch lengths. Just big enough to fit into their woodstove, which was how they heated the house most of the winter. Still, Will was surprised to see his father doing the cutting himself. Usually he had Humberto do the physically challenging work on the farm. Then Will remembered—Humberto was busy this morning.

"Want me to start hauling this toward the shed?" Will shouted over the chain saw's roar.

Mr. Archer looked up at Will through thick plastic safety goggles. Frowning, he turned down the chain saw to a rumble. "What?"

Will gestured toward the shed. "Want me to start piling up the wood?"

"Carl's going to do it," Will's father said. "He's coming over later."

"I'll take care of the glass," Will offered.

"Carl and I will see to it," Mr. Archer said. He looked at Will warily. "You just take it easy."

Will sighed impatiently. "I'm okay."

"Just make sure the animals are fed tonight, and see if you can figure out what's wrong with the gate. You can help me tomorrow. I'm keeping the stand closed for the day, but we have to be open for the weekend. Summer people need their gourmet vegetables."

Will fought the annoyance that grasped at him like a monkey's paw. He appreciated that his father was trying to do him a favor. But it was in his dad's own particular way. Even when his father was being kind to Will, he never lost sight of who came first—the customer. Everything Mr. Archer did was calculated according to a mental profit-and-loss statement.

Will stood and watched his father for a moment. He actually would have preferred to have some work to do, but he didn't want to have to explain why. As it was, the little chores his father had assigned him could be done later, in about an hour. Will started for the house, but when he saw that his mother's car was in the driveway, he took a detour toward the garage. *Can't deal with her right now.*

It took a moment for his eyes to adjust to the darkness in the musty garage. As usual, the first thing he saw was the light wood paddle over his father's rarely used workbench. Skipper Award, it read. Tim had won it from the local sailing club when he was twelve, and Will had always envied it. Tim had been an outstanding sailor . . . and look where it had gotten him.

Will remembered the gentle rocking of the boat as he had stepped into the *Vagabond* beside his brother the night Tim disappeared. The sunlight had glinted off the water. When Will had looked out across the bay, he'd caught sight of a dark shape against the shimmering gold. Before he'd had a chance to call out to Tim, the shape had disappeared. It had looked like a swimmer. But it had been very far out in the bay. *I must have imagined it,* Will had thought then.

And that was what he was starting to think about the girl the day before.

Will tried to shake off the thought, wondering when he would get used to the little land mines planted throughout his life. Everything in Will's life was laced with Tim. His absence was a silent presence that lurked in unexpected corners. Now thoughts of the girl surprised him the same way.

Will hauled out his heavy black Honda motorcycle and pointed it toward the road. He was heading toward the beach.

Maybe there would be something there. Some sign. Some clue.

Something that would say, *She was here.*

Will strapped on his helmet and kicked the bike

to life. He buzzed out the driveway and down the limb-lined road. An orange public works truck was parked on the side, guys in hard hats shoving branches into a portable chipper. Will gave them a wave as he passed and punched the accelerator.

He sped past his family's own field of sunflowers—a customer favorite, surprisingly undamaged in the storm—and two hothouses of organically grown tomatoes and basil. The Archer family had owned farmland in Walfang for over three hundred years. They'd been here when there was nothing but farmers, fishermen, and preachers. Local streets were named for their ancestors—Archer Road, Old Archer Lane. Over the years, parcels of land had been sold off, developed to make enormous mansions with ancient-looking turrets and shingles on the outside, and spacious rooms, cathedral ceilings, and up-to-the minute appliances on the inside. Many of these houses boasted "green" and "eco-friendly" features, which always made Will laugh because, of course, the best way to go green was to not have a nine-thousand-square-foot house that gets used just two months out of the year. As he sped down the quiet side street, Will peered past the high boxwood hedges to catch glimpses of vast emerald-green lawns landscaped with ubiquitous hydrangeas and climbing roses, and he thought about the fertilizer that was spread with abandon, the water needed to keep everything green and lush even in August, the pesticides and sprays. These people's idea of going green was to drive a hybrid car to the local farm stand and buy a few vegetables, then drive home again to eat beside the chlorine-laced pool instead of the beach that was two blocks away.

And the farm stand that they drove to? That was his father's.

Despite the family history, Will's father was no farmer. Of course there were farmers out here. A neighbor down the road—from another family legacy—had gone to Cornell Agricultural School. But Bertrand Archer had no interest in real farming. He owned land, sure, and hired people to plant and harvest the flowers and vegetables. But Bert had figured out that real farming wasn't where the money was. The money was in retail, or in (as Will liked to think of it) his boutique vegetables. People in the Hamptons didn't care how much Bert charged for a pint of tomatoes. If they saw fresh kettle fries being made at a roadside stand, they'd buy them no matter what the cost. If they were looking for a housewarming gift, they'd buy handmade lavender soap or a bouquet of flowers without thinking.

They didn't count the change from their hundred-dollar bills. They signed the AmEx receipt without looking at it. And if Bertrand Archer's farm stand was the most expensive around, well, that must be because it was the best.

And so that was the kind of farming Will's father did—he had enough greenhouses to stock the stand with heirloom varieties, and he grew enough corn to pile on a table near the road. He hired a good-looking local girl to make sweet-potato fries in the late afternoons, so that the smell would waft over customers, hungry from a day at the beach, who had stopped to buy that night's vegetables. He kept ducks and two picturesque black sheep beside the stand, and sold little bags of grain so that children could feed them while their parents shopped. Bertrand grew all of the flowers close to the road, so that people could see the dahlias and sunflowers in their regal glory. He had Humberto and Alma do the picking early in the morning, and then disappear before eight, when the customers started arriving. And he worked the cash register himself, or else had Will or his mom do it. He told jokes and schmoozed, and let everyone know that he was the owner and that this was a family business. He pointed out the scones that his wife had baked, the flowers that he himself had arranged (really, just criticized Alma for not arranging properly). He gave the city folks enough local color so that they felt good about rubbing elbows with the "real" locals—the farmers who had worked this soil for generations. The salt of the earth.

But it was mostly just smoke and mirrors. Will's father was a businessman, not a farmer.

There was nothing wrong with it, Bertrand Archer said. He was just playing a part, like a magician. People came for the show. They wanted to believe. You didn't actually have to learn real magic; you just had to give them what they wanted. So he kept the farming picturesque, and left the dirty work to the suckers.

When Will's father was young, Walfang hadn't been the crazy tourist scene it was today, where a bungalow five blocks from the beach could rent for $10,000 a week. Gretchen's family was technically "summer people," too, since they lived in New York City most of the year. But her grandfather had bought the house in 1944, and Gretchen's dad had grown up spending summers hunting for crabs with Will's dad. So the Ellis family acted like, and were treated more or less like, honorary Walfangers. It always made Will crack up to see his farmer father hanging out with tattooed, ragged-looking Johnny Ellis. *Then again, that must be what people think when they see boring me with Gretchen.*

The beach was lined with workers when Will pulled up to the boardwalk. He parked his bike and trotted down the stairs to the sand. It was crusty and partially dry in the sun, but—judging by how easy it was to walk on—Will guessed it was wet below the surface. A tall figure was photographing a pile of debris stacked near the overturned lifeguard chair.

"Angus," Will called to his friend. "You call this helping?"

"Will!" Angus held up his hand for a high five and drew Will in for a dude hug. "I'm just getting some photos for the paper. They probably won't use any of them, but whatever. Interning at the *Gazette*, man. It's a glamour job. *Pachow, pachow*—make love to the camera." He pretended to take a sexy picture of a washed-up boot. "Shit, can you believe this mess?"

"It's not as bad as I thought it would be," Will admitted.

Angus's wide smile darkened. "Tree branches ain't all they found, bro."

A sudden wave of nausea hit Will. "What?"

Angus's voice dropped. "Man, they found a body. As in a *dead* body."

"A girl?" Will's voice was a hoarse whisper.

"No, man, a guy. He was all torn up, like he'd been caught in a propeller or something. He was shredded, dude." Angus grimaced. "Like he'd been eaten alive."

"Who was it?"

"No clue—and here's the kicker. So I'm, like, all foaming at the mouth to write the story, right? Like, 'Mysterious Death in Walfang!' Byline: Angus McFarlan! But my editor is like, 'No, no. We don't know what killed the guy. It'll freak out the tourists. We'll just keep it on the DL, put it in the police blotter but keep a lid on it.' "

"Does your editor really talk like he's starring in a CW show?"

"Only in translation." Angus grinned.

"So you're not reporting it at all?"

"Just in the obits, man. If we find out who the guy was." Angus looked out over the vast expanse of ocean. The water was surprisingly calm, as if sheepish about the destruction it had caused the night before.

"So—what happened?" Will asked. "I mean, what do you think? Shark?"

Angus shook his head. "Nah. I don't know. The body was *shredded*, man. If it was a shark, I think we would've found less of him, if you know what I mean."

"Crazy."

"And speaking of crazy—did you hear about Kirk Worstler?"

"I saw him downtown earlier." Will skipped the part about how Kirk had stared so hard he'd practically bored a hole in Gretchen's skull. "Why—what's up?"

"He went nuts yesterday and ran up to the fire station and set off the town alarms." Angus opened his eyes comically wide. "The firemen freaked—the whole town freaked. I'm surprised you couldn't hear it."

"God. What happened to that kid?"

"All those Worstlers are nuts, man," Angus said.

"Yeah, I've heard that." Everyone on the island knew it—the Worstlers were crazy. It was the boys, always the boys. Kirk's grandfather Adelai had been a healer of sorts, and his father, Ishmael, was said to speak in tongues. Ishmael's brother had been lost at sea—the story was that he had jumped overboard. And Kirk's father had drunk himself to death. He'd been gone five years, and most said good riddance. He'd been a mean drunk, and he hadn't been kind to Kirk's mother or his sister.

For a long time Kirk had seemed like a normal kid. He'd been sensitive, sure, and artistic. But over the years something had shifted in him. What had for years been curiosity and keen intelligence turned to anxious watchfulness. He spent hours alone, walking the beaches, not playing, like other children, but watching. For a while, after his father's death, he seemed to get better. He seemed like a normal, sad child. But then, after Danny Sawdee's party last year, he changed again. Some people said that he'd taken acid, some said mushrooms. There were even a few who said that Kirk hadn't taken anything at all—he'd had a religious experience, a vision, an awakening. All anyone knew for sure was that Kirk had taken a dare to climb to the top of the abandoned lighthouse at the tip of the island, and after he came down, he was different, and he was never the same again.

There were a couple of freshmen who thought that Kirk had seen an angel. One even said that she'd heard him singing one night. It was the most beautiful song, like it had been sent from heaven. She said that she didn't understand the words, but they sounded foreign.

But most people just thought he was a crazed druggie.

"I heard his sister's been trying to get him into rehab, but his mom says they can't pay for it."

"How do you find out all this crap?"

"Family connections. Besides, I'm a born reporter, man!" Angus laughed. "I live for this shit. And speaking of—" He stooped to capture a photo of a crab scuttling over a pile of seaweed-covered junk. One claw was waving a scrap of paper like an overeager newsboy. "Hey, when's your friend getting back?"

"Gretchen? She's back."

"Really?" Angus grinned. "Well, okay then." He turned back to his pile of wood and seaweed.

Will felt like he should say something more. Something like, *Why are you asking?* But he didn't want to seem like he cared. Because he didn't, of course. Gretchen knew a lot of people on the island—she came here every year. He knew that she and Angus were friendly. But he didn't know what to think of

Angus's grin. He wasn't sure his friend had a shot with Gretchen. He wasn't really her type. Whatever that was.

Honestly, Gretchen dated a lot. She'd had a pretty serious boyfriend last year—Jason something. He was a real summer person type—drove a white Lexus, had the million-dollar smile. Will had only met him a couple of times and privately thought he was a grade-A jerk. Sometimes he thought Gretchen thought so, too. But he was smart and rich, and Gretchen liked going to expensive restaurants and getting surprise presents, so Jason worked for her, Will guessed.

Will looked down the beach. People were dotted here and there, collecting garbage and placing it in large contractor bags. The detritus was disappearing at a rapid pace. Will expected that it would be in its usual pristine state by Friday, when the first migrants from New York made their way east on the Jitney.

Will caught sight of a long-haired girl at the end of the beach. She was bent over a large piece of driftwood. Black hair spilled over her shoulders, and reflexively Will grabbed Angus's arm. "Dude—who's that?"

"What? Who?" His eyes focused on the heavyset bald guy with the clipboard and tight button-down short-sleeved sport shirt. "Franklin Overmeyer? He's with the mayor's office."

"No." Will's heart was racing. "That girl with the long hair."

"Kate Sands?"

At that moment the girl turned slightly, and Will got a proper view of her face. She had brown eyes, not green, and her face was round and freckled. It wasn't the girl from yesterday. It was a girl from his Spanish class. "Oh—I . . . I thought she was someone else."

"Dude, are you diggin' on Kate? Because she's a *Gazette* intern, too. I could put in a word—"

"No, seriously. I thought she was someone else."

Angus waggled his eyebrows, and Will sighed. "Hey, look, I've got to head, okay? I'll see you?"

Now I'm seeing things, Will thought as he walked away. *Ghosts of the girl from hurricanes past.* He felt as if the beach were littered with them.

Chapter Four

From the Walfang Gazette
Police Blotter: Drowning Death of New York City Man Ruled a Suicide

Fifty-six-year-old Terrance "Terry" Milton died on Wednesday as a result of an apparent suicide. He maintained a summer house close to where his body was found Thursday morning. Neighbors state that Mr. Milton had been depressed since the death of his mother last year. . . .

"Will! You're just in time!" his father said as Will came down the stairs. "Come try some of this wine. This is Mr. Jameson—he has a vineyard on the North Fork. We're thinking of selling some at the stand."

Will's mother sat silently on the couch, sipping from a glass of pale amber liquid.

"Don't you need a liquor license for that?" Will asked as he shook his head at the wine. "No thanks."

"You probably wouldn't need a license to take orders," Mr. Jameson said. He was handsome in an aging-daytime-TV-star kind of way: tall, gray hair slicked back, tanned skin, brilliant smile. "We're still working everything out, but it looks like we can offer same-day delivery."

"People are going to go nuts for this sauvignon

blanc," Will's dad said. "Are you sure you don't want some, Will?"

"It's really delicious," his mother said quietly.

"I'm about to hop on the bike," Will told them.

"One sip?" Mr. Jameson laughed.

Will just smiled a tight smile. The truth was, he hated wine. Beer, too. But he didn't want to explain that to Mr. Former Soap Opera Star.

"My teetotaler son." Will's dad rolled his eyes. "Where are you headed?"

"Just into town."

"You remember you're working a shift later?" Mrs. Archer asked.

"How could I forget?"

Mr. Archer waved his hand at his son and said, "Go on, get out of here! Have fun!" He gave a false, hearty laugh that made Will want to be sick. Will waved and headed for the motorcycle. He yanked on his helmet and kicked the bike to life. It started with a roar, and Will revved it a couple of times before pulling out of the driveway.

He tore up the road, breathing easier with every inch of space between himself and his father. Will resented the elaborate act Mr. Archer put on for others. He didn't understand it. And it made him furious that the act seemed to take up all of his father's energy. He barely spoke to Will when they were alone.

Will parked the bike and stored his helmet, then made his way over to the storefront. He stared at the sign on the door for a long moment, tracing the ornate gold letters with his eyes: Worthington's Fine Antiques. Will ran his thumb beneath the wide canvas strap slung across his chest, hitching his messenger bag higher onto his shoulder. He caught a glimpse of his face in the glass door. Beneath his tan, his complexion seemed dull and gray. His night had been filled with dreams. He'd been surfing with Tim, laughing and tumbling in the waves. It wasn't until he woke up that the dream seemed nightmarish. Tim was dead, and somewhere perhaps a green-eyed girl was, too.

Finally Will touched the brass handle and pushed his way in.

The proprietor, an older gentleman, was arranging something in a glass display case as Will stepped into the cool, dim store. The man popped his head over the edge of the counter. "I'll be right with you," he said, then disappeared again into his antiques-lined gopher hole.

Will took the opportunity to look around the store. To his left was a large desk. It was ornately carved with the heads of lions and other exotic animals. The feet were bird claws clutching round balls. The desk was enormous, and was designed so that people could sit at either side. Fascinated, Will inspected it from all angles.

"It's a nineteenth-century partners desk," the man explained, coming up behind Will. "They could face each other and argue over budget items, presumably."

"There's no price on it," Will pointed out.

"This item sells for forty thousand dollars," the man said.

Will laughed. "Well, I guess it's good I already have a desk."

The owner smiled, which made his prim appearance seem more approachable. Now he was just a lanky man with tiny round bifocals and khaki pants, rather than the proprietor of the kind of store that sold desks that cost more than Will's father's car. "Is there something I can help you with?"

"Well . . ." Will dug in his bag and pulled out something wrapped in a brown paper bag. The man peered closely as Will gently removed the flute and held it out for inspection. "Do you know anything about this? There's one like it in your window." Will gestured over his shoulder.

The man scurried behind the counter and yanked on a pair of white cotton gloves. Then he reached for the flute and handled it very carefully. "This instrument is quite an antique."

"How old?"

"I'm not sure. I'd have to have it authenticated, of course, but it could be as much as five hundred years old. Are you looking to sell it?"

"No." The mere question made Will's palms itch. He wanted that flute back, but didn't want to snatch it from the man's hands. "I just—I just want to know more about it."

"I'm sorry I can't tell you much. The one in the window is extremely rare. In fact, I'm just waiting for some authentication documents so that it can be shipped to its new home in a museum in Nice, France." He took the flute to the counter and set it down gently.

Then he came up with a cloth sack. The man gingerly dropped the flute into the sack, then rolled it back up. He handed it to Will. "Something this precious should be protected," the man said.

"Thanks." Will tucked the flute back into his bag, feeling embarrassed about the crumpled paper bag. "Can you at least tell me where you got the other one?"

"Interestingly, that was also from a young person. She works right next door." The man scribbled something onto the back of a business card. *ASIA MARIN*, read the all-capital scrawl.

"She works at Bella's?" Will asked, surprised at this piece of luck. "That's great—I'm headed there, anyway."

"The hand of fate," the man intoned.

Will nodded, amused at how quickly the gentleman's primness had returned. "Maybe so."

Will settled into a two-person booth and set his gray messenger bag gently on the table. It was late morning, and the early lunch crowd was starting to trickle in. Gretchen had told Will that she'd been stuck with mostly lunch shifts, but he wasn't sure she was working today. He surveyed the long space. Men in farmer caps, huddled in their booths, were bent close over fish and chips. Two fat women laughed over a shared banana split. Everywhere, people were talking and eating. *Just like normal life,* Will thought.

Will pulled the flute from his bag, then carefully stripped it of its wrappings. He supposed he should be wearing gloves like the man in the antiques store, but he'd already held the flute a hundred times, so he couldn't see what difference it would make now. The wood was light in his hand, like the bone of a bird.

It had been Tim's flute. Not that Tim played the flute. As far as Will knew, his brother had played only the guitar. Nevertheless, this was Tim's flute. At least, Will thought of it that way.

Weeks after his family installed a headstone over an empty box, Angus's uncle had called Will down to the station. He said he had something for him. When Will arrived, Police Chief Barry McFarlan had pulled a plastic evidence bag from his desk drawer. He explained that the officer called to the scene of Tim's death had found the flute on the boat, wedged into the rigging. It didn't seem to have any bearing on the case, so they could let it go. "I know Tim was really into music. It must have been his," Barry said, and asked Will if he wanted it, "as a memento."

A memento, Will had thought. *A memento of my brother's death.* As if he didn't have enough of those. Still, he'd taken the flute. Then he'd slipped it into his bottom drawer—the one he never opened—and forgotten about it until a couple of days ago. He knew it was crazy to think that the flute had anything to do with his brother. Still, it was connected simply by proximity. And when Will had spotted its twin, or at least its cousin, in the store window, he'd decided to find out something about it.

Will surveyed the diner, but he didn't see Gretchen anywhere. A punk-nerd waitress with rag doll hair and a gray uniform was joking with a table of old ladies.

The short-order cook—Angel, a Bella's fixture from the beginning of Will's memory—was at his place behind the stove. Will could see him through the food-delivery window. Wondering if the punk girl could be Asia, he picked up a newspaper that someone had left on the seat. He scanned the front page, then the back page. The front page of the local news section, with its obituaries and police blotter. He found a short mention of the body Angus had told Will about at the beginning of the week, but nothing about a dark-haired girl. Will conjured her in his mind and was surprised at just how clearly he could see her green sea-glass eyes, her pale skin, her high cheekbones. The way her black hair streamed behind her like ribbons as she waded into the sea.

The whole scene had an air of unreality to it. No girl could be that beautiful. No one would wade into a violent ocean during a storm. It was like one of those nightmares that seem so real they leave you gasping with relief when you wake up and find yourself surrounded by your own walls, sleeping in your own bed.

"What would you like?"

Will looked up, and his heart froze. It didn't just stop, it felt cold and fragile, as if a single tap could break it.

It's her.

Luminous green eyes were trained on his face, and her black hair was tied in a knot at the back of her neck. She was wearing the standard dreary waitress uniform and had a pencil tucked behind her ear, but still, she seemed too beautiful to be real.

"Are you all right?" she asked in a voice that fogged

his mind. Will knew that he had to say something, but he couldn't find words. "A Coke," he choked out finally.

She wrote that down. When she looked up again, her head tilted slightly. *Does she recognize me, too?*

The waitress glanced down at the table, and her expression changed. "Where did you get this?" she asked. Her voice was careful, her eyes guarded.

Will looked down at his hands, which were still holding the wooden flute. His mind felt like a scrambled radio signal—he couldn't make sense of words. He didn't know what to tell her. *"It may have belonged to my dead brother"? "A cop gave it to me as a memento"?* Finally his eyes landed on her name tag.

"Asia Marin," Will said aloud.

Asia cocked her head again, as if she suspected that Will was pulling an elaborate joke—one she didn't like much. "Do I know you?"

Will wasn't sure how to answer that. *Don't you?* he wanted to ask. *I nearly ran you over, then tried to stop your suicide in the sea, remember?*

"No," Will said at last. "I, uh—the man in the antiques store next door sent me. He said that you'd sold him a flute like this one."

Asia slipped into the seat across from Will's. She took the flute from him with delicate fingers and studied the instrument. "Very similar, yes," she admitted.

She was sitting so close that Will could practically feel her breath. He was stunned at how silken her voice was. It was something to wrap yourself in. "I'm no expert. . . ." She looked at him, her eyes wary.

"This isn't *Antiques Roadshow,*" Will told her. "Just—anything you can tell me. This flute's a complete mystery." He pretended to lean closer to have a look at the flute, but really, he just wanted to be closer to this gorgeous girl.

"Well . . . technically, this isn't a flute. When it has holes like this, it's called a recorder." A slender finger indicated the rough-hewn holes. "I think this is probably European. And it's old—as old as the one I had, maybe older. It could be four or five hundred years old. I think it's pretty hard to date these things."

"How did you get yours?" Will asked.

"It was a gift."

"So why did you sell it?"

"I had no further use for it." Asia's eyes narrowed, as if Will had stepped to the edge of dangerous waters. "Are you asking about my flute or yours?"

"Sorry. Mine. What kind of wood is it?" Will asked.

Asia's eyes met his. "Not wood," she told him. "Bone."

A tiny shiver went through him, as if the temperature in the diner had dropped ten degrees.

"Asia!" Angel bellowed from the kitchen. "Am I paying you to sit on your butt all day?"

"Oh, are we getting paid?" called out the nerd-punk waitress. Her old-lady customers cackled gleefully.

"I'd better go get your Coke," Asia said. She placed the flute gently atop its cloth bag and stood up. "I'll be back in a moment."

Will just nodded, still partially dazed. Her beauty

and her mellifluous voice had left him so dazzled that he'd completely forgotten to ask Asia where her flute had come from. He hadn't managed to ask her why—or even if—she'd walked into the sea. *I'll ask her when she comes back,* Will thought. But when his Coke arrived, it was the nerd-punk waitress who delivered it.

"Is Asia on break?" Will asked.

The waitress just gave him a look, as if she was used to guys asking about Asia. "Yeah," she said, half wary, half bored.

Will drank his Coke, then looked at his watch. He had to get to the farm stand; it was time for his shift. He couldn't wait for Asia forever.

Now that he'd found her, he'd just have to find her again later. *At least she's real.*

That thought should have been more comforting than it was.

"Hey, toots, that old lady in the corner is snapping in your general direction." Lisette's arms were piled with lunch platters for table four, so she pursed her goth-painted lips in the direction of one of Gretchen's booths. Lisette was in her mid-twenties, but she talked like someone from the 1960s. She wore horn-rimmed glasses over brown eyes rimmed in dark blue eye shadow. Her hair was an extremely unlikely shade of red reminiscent of Raggedy Ann, and today she had it spouting like a small fountain from the top of her head. She'd worked at Bella's for three years and had her pet regulars, like the guys from the security company at table four. "I've seen that old witch in here before. You'd better get over there before she turns you into a frog, sweets."

"Lisette, am I paying you to chat with Gretchen?" Angel O'Rourke—Bella's short-order cook and manager—scowled, twitching his orange moustache into a frown. Gretchen liked to think of him as the Irish-Dominican version of Oscar the Grouch.

"Oh, go flip something, Angel," Lisette shot back before taking off toward her table.

Gretchen slapped her sketch pad closed and looked over at the woman in the corner. She was heavyset, with hair that was a wild mess of gray frosted with three different shades of blond. Her face was like a wrinkled sheet spread over a fluffy featherbed, and her frowning lips were outlined in bright pink. *Snap, snap, snap.* Once she realized that she had Gretchen's attention, the woman held up her coffee mug and tapped it with a hot-pink nail.

Gretchen hurried over.

"This coffee is cold." The woman set it down primly on the paper placemat that sat on the gold-flecked Formica table.

Gretchen took the mug—surprisingly warm—from the woman's hands.

"And it tastes old. You might want to brew up a fresh batch." The woman looked down at the newspaper that was spread open across her table.

"This batch was brewed five minutes before I served it to you," Gretchen protested.

Frosty the Hairstyle shot her a withering look.

"Then you'd better get a new brand, because that stuff tastes like battery acid."

Gretchen felt a flame of anger rise in her chest. She was just about to snap at the customer when she felt a cool hand, like a gentle splash of water, at her elbow.

"Everything okay here?" asked a silken voice. Asia's steady gaze landed on the woman, who seemed to retreat a little, like a turtle into its shell. "Hello, Mrs. Cuthbert," Asia purred. "How are you feeling today?"

There was something about Asia's stillness that gave Gretchen a sense of vertigo, as if she were staring up at Asia from a great distance. And yet the other waitress wasn't particularly tall. She was just very still. With her long dark hair pinned back in a bun and her fine features, she looked like a Greek statue.

"My knee is still bothering me," Mrs. Cuthbert admitted. Her expression turned into a sulky pout. "I was up all night with it."

Asia leaned over and whispered something into Mrs. Cuthbert's ear—or maybe she didn't. Gretchen didn't see Asia's lips move. But the old woman smiled slightly.

"Thank you, dear." She glanced at Gretchen, but the claws had retracted from her eyes.

Wordlessly Asia took the mug and steered Gretchen—still tense from the expectation of a fight—away from the table.

When Gretchen looked back over her shoulder, she saw that Mrs. Cuthbert was gazing out the window. She was smiling faintly, her head swaying back and forth slightly, as if she were bending with a breeze that no one else could feel.

Asia headed behind the counter.

"Are you going to toss that coffee? There's nothing wrong with it," Gretchen told her. "I just brewed it. And it's still hot." Bella's was known for its coffee—delicious and always brewed to be melt-your-lips-off strong.

Asia nodded, smiling softly. "Yes, I know."

"Then—?"

"I'm just going to stand here, count to sixty, and then bring her the same mug all over again. She'll be happy with it this time." Gretchen looked doubtful, but Asia gave her a confident smile and touched her on the arm. "You'll see."

Gretchen watched as Asia made her way to Mrs. Cuthbert's table. The old woman turned away from the window to pick up the mug. She took a sip, then smiled up at Asia.

"Is Asia charming the cobras again?" Lisette asked as she reached behind the counter for a yellow squeeze bottle of mustard.

"It looks like it," Gretchen admitted.

"That girl could charm the cute right out of a Cabbage Patch Kid." Lisette rolled her eyes as she held the mustard aloft. "All right, keep your pants on," she called to one of the guys at table four, who had just hollered that his burger was getting cold.

The bell behind Gretchen rang. "Table seven, order up," Angel called.

Gretchen stifled a groan. Seven was Mrs. Cuthbert's table. Gretchen half expected her to put up a fight about the quality of the sandwich, but Mrs. Cuthbert's mood had clearly shifted. "Thank you, dear," she said pleasantly as Gretchen set the platter on the table.

Surprised, Gretchen mumbled an awkward "you're welcome" and retreated. Since Bella's was half empty—it was three forty-five—Gretchen wiped down the countertops. Then she filled the paper napkin dispensers. Then she sorted cutlery. And when all of that was done, she went back to her sketch. She wanted to capture the interlocking spiderweb of wrinkles on Ms. Cuthbert's neck. The way they danced as she ate was fascinating. . . .

"Beautiful."

Gretchen started again. "I need to get a bell to put around your neck," she told Asia, who was peering over her shoulder at the sketch.

Asia smiled. Her fingers traced the drawing lightly, the touch too delicate to smudge the work. She reached for the sketchbook, then hesitated. "May I?" She flipped through several sketches, studying each a moment, then moving on. Most people looked through her book with limited attention, like they were flipping though a magazine. But Asia really seemed to be studying each drawing. She came to a portrait and stopped. "I know this person, I think."

"No."

Asia's eyebrows lifted, and Gretchen felt like a fool. She knew her voice had come out harsher than she'd intended. "It's just—this is a picture of someone. . . ." She couldn't say it. A thousand emotions threatened to overwhelm her—rage, pain, love, fear.

"Someone . . ." Asia studied her face. "Gone."

Gretchen nodded.

Asia let the words hang in the air. After a moment, Gretchen could almost feel them floating away. She inhaled.

Asia looked down at the sketch—at Tim's grinning face. Gretchen studied the portrait of Tim, with the almost-too-long nose, the straight teeth, the shaggy hair. She'd drawn it at the beginning of last summer, before he'd had a chance to buzz his locks. Before he vanished.

"I do know him," Asia said. Her voice was low, almost a murmur, like the babble of a brook running over rocks. Her finger traced the edge of the paper. "There was someone who looked like this, who came into the restaurant. But with a scar." She traced a line from her temple to her cheekbone. "Here."

"That's Will." *Asia met Will?* Gretchen shifted uncomfortably. "He's—" There were many things that Gretchen could have said here, but she chose, "This picture is of his brother."

Asia nodded. She didn't ask any of the usual questions: *What happened? How did he die? Was he sick? Were they close? How did you know them?* She just sat with Gretchen. Normally Gretchen hated those questions. But, somehow, having them just sit there unasked was worse. Almost involuntarily: "It was an accident. Tim drowned last year."

"You were there." It wasn't a question.

"No." Gretchen's voice wavered. "Will was, though."

"What happened?"

"Nobody knows."

Asia tilted her head, looking at Gretchen carefully.

"Will can't remember. And the body was never found."

Asia took a moment to digest this piece of information. "Sorrow," she said.

It was such a strange thing to say. *Sorrow.* Yes, that was what she felt, in many different ways. Overwhelming sorrow.

With deliberate slowness, Asia turned to the next drawing.

"Do you like art?" Gretchen asked suddenly.

"Doesn't everyone like art?" Asia asked.

"Not really." Gretchen shrugged. "That is, a lot of people aren't very interested in it. People our age, especially." This was one of the reasons that she found it so hard to talk to the girls in her prep school in New York City. None of them was interested in the things she was interested in. Frankly, most of them didn't seem interested in *anything.*

Asia seemed to absorb Gretchen's comment for a moment. "True. I suppose not everyone likes all art. But everyone likes some kind of art—dance, music, movies . . ."

"I guess I meant visual art."

Asia smiled, and Gretchen studied her face. *She is charming, that's for sure,* Gretchen thought. It was more than just the fact that she had taken care of

Gretchen's angry customer. There was something in her voice, in her fluid manner, that made people feel relaxed around her. For some reason, Gretchen felt as if she knew Asia. Yet there was something a little reserved about her. Gretchen felt a coldness radiating off her, like vapor from dry ice.

"Were you thinking of some particular visual art?" Asia asked.

"There's an exhibit at the Miller," Gretchen said. The Miller Gallery was the tiny local gallery that often showed surprisingly excellent work. It featured local artists, which—out here—meant world-renowned artists. The list of luminaries who had started their careers there was bright enough to light the eastern seaboard. "'Gifts of the Sea,' it's called. It's terrific. I went there the other day. You should check it out."

"Perhaps I will," Asia said. She passed by Gretchen on her way to take a plate from Angel, and her physical presence gave Gretchen a shiver.

There's definitely something cold about her, Gretchen decided. *Cold as the bottom of the sea.*

Chapter Five

From the Walfang Gazette
Local Boy Breaks Into First Church

A local boy is accused of breaking into First Church on Dune Avenue yesterday. "I don't know how he got in," said the church administrator, Marion Wheeler. "But he didn't harm anything. I just came running when I heard the music." According to witnesses, Kirk Worstler, 15, climbed into the balcony to play the church organ. "I didn't even know he could play the organ," said Adelaide Worstler, Kirk's older sister. "But he seemed to know what he was doing. I had to drag him out of there."

"Don't eat the merchandise," Will told Gretchen as she popped a blackberry into her mouth. Will shoved his finger into a pod and let the heavy beans fall into the aluminum bowl with a gentle *ping-ping-ping.* Shelled beans meant more money, just like washed mesclun greens versus straight from the field. *Prep work is for peons, like me.*

"I'm buying this," Gretchen insisted as she took another blackberry from the stained paper crate. She grinned impishly. The dark juice had stained the edges of her teeth purple. A breeze ruffled her wild dandelion hair, and for a moment Will could see the six-year-old Gretchen again.

"When was the last time you bought anything from this stand?" Will demanded.

"It's not my fault that your father never lets us pay." She picked up a large box of golden cherry tomatoes and placed it in a shallow cardboard tray next to the blackberries. "These are like candy," she said as she popped one into her mouth.

"They're my favorites." The golden tomatoes grew fat and sweet, as if they'd soaked up the flavor of the sun. The heavy rain had caused a few to split, their sweetness calling the fruit flies to come feast. Will knew that they would have to sell them fast.

Gretchen leaned down and patted Guernsey, Will's old black Lab, who was curled up in her usual spot beneath the wood table that held the cash register, fresh honey supplied by a local apiary, and stick candy. Guernsey lifted her dark eyes and sniffed Gretchen's hand, then tucked her head back onto her foreleg and went back to drowsing.

"Sweet old thing," Gretchen said.

Guernsey didn't deny it.

Gravel crunched as a beat-up Ford rolled into the lot. It was late afternoon, and folks had been trickling in all day. Usually the farm stand was busy early—the caffeinated type A personalities liked to shop for freshly baked scones and fruit at seven in the morning. It would stay quiet until four-thirty, when the cocktail crowd started to appear, looking for something to serve alongside their artisanal cheeses and imported crackers, and gourmet cooks would frown over arugula and thump cantaloupes.

But this was no epicure coming to inspect peaches. "Great," Will said as long legs unfolded from the tiny silver car. "Another freeloader."

"Hey!" Angus called as he loped over toward them. When he saw Gretchen, he ran a hand through his bushy brown hair. "Where have you people been hiding?"

"Angus!" Gretchen waved, and Angus's face lit up like something that had just been plugged in. "You have to try one of these."

Angus was about to protest, but she popped a cherry tomato into his mouth. "You're doing tastings now?" Angus teased.

"Will never gives anything away for free, but these are mine," Gretchen told him. "Have a blackberry."

Angus opened his mouth and let her feed him again. He smiled at her as he chewed.

"We rinse off all the manure before we put the stuff out," Will told him.

Gretchen rolled her eyes, but Angus looked a little unsure.

"Kidding," Will told him. "We don't rinse anything."

"*Wi-ill.*" Gretchen stretched his name to two syllables. It was her complaining voice. "Ignore him, Angus. Want more?" She held out the box of fat, glossy blackberries.

"Um, no thanks," Angus told her. He hopped onto the wide wooden table and sat down. "Listen, I actually came over to invite you guys to a party."

"Your mom is unbarring the gates?" Will asked.

"No way, dude. Not after what happened last year—my place is in lockdown until graduation. But Ansell's having a thing. Next Friday."

"On his beach?" Gretchen asked, and Angus nodded. "Sweet."

Harry Ansell was rich. Seriously rich. But his parents did a lot for the town, so the regular Walfangers didn't completely despise them. Will knew Harry and didn't think he was a bad guy. Not the brightest, but not horrible.

"I'll drive," Gretchen volunteered, looking at Will.

"I'm not coming."

"Yes, you are."

Will shook his head and glanced over at Angus, who was watching the argument with amusement. Gretchen didn't seem to understand that Will wasn't like her. He couldn't just go to parties and act happy all the time. Sometimes, being near people made him feel like he was going to break apart. Okay, sure, he had to work at the stand. His family needed him. But he didn't have to go to a party and pretend to drink vile beer and endure everyone's sympathetic looks and sad murmurs.

"You're coming."

"No."

"Okay, I'm glad we've discussed this. I'll pick you up at nine."

"Forget it, Gretchen."

Gretchen just smiled and took her tray of half-eaten blackberries, tomatoes, and lettuce. "Thanks for the invite, Angus. See you! And remember, Will—nine on Friday."

"Gretchen, I'm not—"

But she was sashaying away, singing at the top of her lungs. Her long Indian skirt swayed as she walked. Her hair hung halfway down her tan back, barely skimming the top of her lavender halter.

"She's so freakin' hot," Angus said, half to himself. Then he sighed and turned back to Will. "Hey, dude, so I checked with my uncle."

"Which uncle?"

"Barry."

"Right."

"The police chief. About the . . ." He dropped his voice to a dramatic whisper. "Dead body." He stared at Will with wide brown eyes.

"And?"

"He wouldn't tell me anything."

Will snorted and went back to shelling beans.

"But don't you think that's weird?"

"That the police chief wouldn't tell the biggest gossip in town details of a murder case? Um, not really."

"Dude, he's my *uncle.* I'm telling you—something's going on. This is like that whole deal in *Jaws* where nobody wants to freak out the tourists, but there's this giant shark just, like, *out there.* And it's just *waiting* and *planning* and hoping for a tasty snack."

"Is it mechanical and made of rubber?"

"Dude." Angus shook his head. "I'm telling you. Something's up. This town has secrets." He hopped off the table. "And I'm going to find them out."

"Maybe your uncle is trying to protect you."

"Whose side are you on? I don't need protection. I need answers." He waved over his shoulder as he walked back to his car. The salt had gotten to it near the bottom, and orange rust was making its way up the car in a pattern that looked like a gentle wave. "I'll see you at Ansell's party, if not before!" he called as he folded himself up into his little clown car.

Will didn't even bother shouting that he wasn't going to Ansell's. *Nobody listens to me, anyway.*

"So then I was like, 'Nice wedding ring,' and I thought he was going to *die,*" Trina said as she rubbed SPF 15 on her legs. "Gia just about fell on the floor laughing, and the guy just sort of crept away like a lizard. I kind of felt bad for him, but, like, don't hit on seventeen-year-olds while you're wearing your evidence, you know?" She spread lotion over her bronze arms and twisted her long brown hair into a clip. Trina was short, but she had lush curves, thick hair, and golden skin that attracted a lot of attention. "What an imbecile."

Gretchen made a small *hm* noise that she hoped would make it sound as if she was still awake. Trina went to her school, and they used to be close friends. But lately all of Trina's stories seemed to revolve around partying and the guys who were desperate to get with her. Whenever Gretchen listened to her, she felt irritated, so she didn't listen very much.

Gretchen adjusted her sunglasses and looked out over the crashing waves. They were pretty large for the

Atlantic. Their rhythm seemed to beckon to her cheerfully, but Gretchen wasn't fooled. It was still early in the season; the water would be cold.

Will could never understand why Gretchen refused to go into the ocean. She liked the beach, but not the water.

Tim had always teased Gretchen for not even wanting to go into the bay near their house. Her nanny had frightened her about it when Gretchen was a child, and she maintained a superstitious distance from the calm water. Gretchen remembered the day—she and Will must have been about eight or nine—that they took a rowboat out onto the water. It was a battered old craft that had floated up onto their property from the bay during a storm. Tim had adopted it right away and spent time repairing it. He'd even saved up money to replace the oars that were lost. Before they pushed away from the shore, Gretchen had begged to be allowed to row. So Tim took one side and Gretchen took the other, while Will sat across from them, trailing a lazy hand in the water. Tim was bigger than Gretchen, and their oar strength was unequal. It was soon clear that unless one of them gave up their seat, they would do nothing but row around in circles all day. But Gretchen had refused to give up her seat, and Tim wouldn't, either, since he had done all the repairs on the boat. The argument escalated until Tim—in a fit of playful frustration—had tossed Gretchen overboard.

She'd thrashed madly, like a carp on a line, and Tim had laughed until Will shouted, "She means it! Tim, she means it!" Will had held out an oar, but

Gretchen was so terrified that she batted at it, smacking it away from her with a dull thunk. Her screams were choked back by the salt water, her body white-hot with terror. "Shit," Tim hissed, just before he kicked off his shoes and jumped in after her. Somehow he managed to get hold of her and wrap his long arms around her, pinning her arms to her side. "I've got you, I've got you," Tim said as Will held out the oar. He pulled them both to safety. When a red-eyed Gretchen had slopped, wet and dripping, into the house, Johnny had called the Archers for an explanation. Tim had sheepishly confessed, and offered a sincere apology to Gretchen. But Gretchen wouldn't even come to the phone. She didn't speak to Tim for a whole week—even when, in a fit of desperation, he'd sent Will over to talk some sense into Gretchen. "Tim thinks it's funny," Gretchen had told Will. "But feeling scared isn't funny."

Will had made Tim promise not to make fun of her fears, and he swore he would never push her into the water again. And, eventually, that was good enough. After avoiding them for a week, one day Gretchen joined them as they scrounged for wild blueberries at the edge of the property. And the rowboat incident was never mentioned again. The boat washed away in a storm three summers later and wasn't missed at all.

Trina laughed, breaking into Gretchen's thoughts. Gretchen forced herself to smile. "That's funny," she said, with no idea what she was talking about.

"I know!"

Trina babbled on, and Gretchen squirted a blob of white lotion onto her hand.

Gretchen's cell phone buzzed. She wiped the sunblock onto her thigh in a smear and picked up the phone. "Sorry, just a sec."

A text: *Need help spreading that around?*

Gretchen looked up, scanning the public beach. She was used to the deserted waters of the bay near her property and so she felt almost overwhelmed by the number of people nearby, even though it was only eleven in the morning and the beach wasn't very crowded yet. A tall lifeguard chair towered over various groups scattered across the white sand in beach-blanket clumps. Here was a family with picture-perfect children, there were two thick older women in full makeup and gold jewelry stacked up their arms, a rowdy group of extended family, three tan girls in bikinis . . .

Finally she saw him. The ice-blue eyes beneath the pale blond, almost white hair. He was tanned, and his defined muscles ripped down his chest, disappearing into a pair of low-slung, baggy olive trunks. Jason was holding a BlackBerry, and he looked just as good to her as he had last summer.

He was there with a couple of his guy friends. She knew them vaguely—the one with the red hair was Kurt, the dark-skinned one with striking green eyes was Alex, the funny one was Josh. They were horsing around, making a big show of tossing a football, and glancing over to see if the bikini girls had noticed.

Gretchen texted back: *Don't trust u.*

Jason grinned at her and tucked the BlackBerry into a bag. Then he stood up.

Trina caught sight of the handsome specimen walking toward them. She checked out Jason over the tops of her sunglasses. "Who is *that*?" she asked.

"My ex," Gretchen told her.

"Oh."

Jason dropped to the sand beside Gretchen. He touched her hair, weighing it in his hand like a measure of ribbon. "Hey, gorgeous."

"Hey." Gretchen forgot everything she had ever learned about hair being dead tissue. She could have sworn that she had nerves in the tips of her blond strands—she could feel the weight, the warmth of his fingers. "Jason, this is Trina."

"Hi." Trina flashed her man-killing smile. "Great to meet you."

But Jason seemed impervious. "Same," he said, and nodded at her briefly. Then he turned his attention back to Gretchen. "How's the city?" That was how everyone out here referred to New York. It was just "the city." As if they lived in Oz, and there was only one city in the whole world.

"Seems far away," Gretchen told him. "How's Arlington?"

Jason picked up some sand, let it sift through his fingers. "Stupid."

"Yeah." Gretchen knew what he meant. Jason lived with his father most of the year, and they didn't exactly get along. He spent the summers in nearby

Montauk, with his mother. She owned a well-known gallery in New York, and Jason would have preferred to live with her. But his dad was president of a popular gaming company, and he'd managed to hire better lawyers for the divorce. So he'd gotten custody. Jason and Gretchen made a good pair that way—both with absentee mothers.

"I won't be there much longer, though," Jason went on. "I'm heading to Dartmouth in the fall." He dragged his fingers through the sand.

"Lucky," Gretchen told him. "I've got another year."

"Yeah, but you're in the city."

"Yeah." She didn't bother correcting him. It wasn't that she dreaded living out here, going to the public high school instead of the all-girls academy she'd attended in Manhattan for the past eleven years. It was just that she didn't want Trina to text the news to everyone in their class.

Absently she smeared the lotion onto her leg, working it into the skin.

Jason reached out a finger, tracing it along the outer edge of her thigh. Gretchen's eyes locked with his. The heat from the sun made her dizzy.

"Arlington? Isn't that in Virginia?" Trina asked. "Close to D.C.?"

Jason and Gretchen turned to her. Honestly, Gretchen had momentarily forgotten Trina even existed.

"Yeah," Jason said after a beat. "You'd think that would make it kind of interesting, but the place is all lawyers."

"My mother's a lawyer," Trina said.

Jason laughed. "Then you know what I'm talking about."

That's so Jason, Gretchen thought. He never held back. Sometimes it irked her, but mostly it amused her. She respected the fact that Jason truly didn't give a damn what other people thought of him. *I wish I could stop caring about stuff like that.*

Jason turned to Gretchen. "Hey, I'm dying of thirst. Want to come with me to that snack place?"

Gretchen read his gaze. The snack shack wasn't far. It was a large, tasteful building that also had showers and restrooms. It was on an elevated wooden platform, which made it easy to get below the building, where it was cool and dark, and lined with soft sand.

She could already feel his warm hands skimming her sides, sliding over her flat belly. She remembered the way his fingers would twine through her hair. She knew the salty taste of his lips. He hadn't called since last summer, although he'd texted a couple of times and sent her a couple of Facebook messages. But that was the way summer flings went, right? It wasn't like she was looking for true love.

"Sure," Gretchen told him.

"Hey, get me a Diet Pepsi, would you?" Trina called as they started off. A smug little smile curled on her lips, and she looked down at the book in her lap.

Jason and Gretchen exchanged a look. That wasn't exactly the sort of snack they were going for, and

Trina probably knew it. Gretchen blushed and looked away.

"Sure, Trina," Jason said smoothly. "No problem."

Will checked the time on his cell phone. This was typical Angus. Twenty minutes late, and no call, no text.

And he's the one who wanted to go to this stupid show. Will looked up at the brick façade of the Miller Gallery. He'd made the mistake of mentioning that Gretchen had said this "Gifts of the Sea" show was really amazing, and of course Angus had jumped all over it. "We have to go, dude!" Angus had said. "Dude, I love art!"

Even at the time, Will knew that Angus was only saying that because he was digging on Gretchen. Still, Will had been curious about the show. The way Gretchen described it made it sound really interesting. It was by a bunch of different artists, so it wouldn't just be the same beach scene over and over. So he'd said, "Okay. Sure, Angus, let's go." And now Angus was nowhere to be seen.

Will's cell phone buzzed.

Dude, read the text, *stuck at Gaz rewriting story on town dump. Got to skip art. Sorry, A.*

Will sighed. This was why nice guys always got screwed. He texted back, *I'll bring you a seashell.* What was the point of going ballistic on Angus? The guy wasn't going to change.

Now what? Will hesitated. *Am I really the kind of guy who goes to an art show by myself?* he thought.

There was something that seemed kind of pretentious about it. Then again, he'd rather be the kind of guy who looked at art than the kind of guy who *didn't* look at art because he was worried about what it said about him. *I'm overthinking this.* He started up the marble steps.

The glossy dark wood floorboards creaked beneath his sneakers as he walked in. Large skylights sent light pouring onto the white walls and gray trim. Admission to the gallery was free, but Will shoved a few dollar bills into the waist-high Lucite box near the entrance. The gray-haired volunteer behind the counter nodded at him in approval as he passed into the gallery.

There was one other figure inside. She was in profile, and as the bright skylight illuminated the fair skin and dark hair, for a moment Will mistook her for part of the exhibit. Asia seemed carved of stone. *Could someone that delicate scale a bunch of rocks like a human spider?*

He hung back a moment, unsure whether to join her. She hadn't been warm toward him the other day, and she'd bailed when he started asking questions. Part of him wanted to turn and scurry away. But another part of him had clearly already made a decision, because he found himself moving across the squeaking floorboards toward her. He felt like an elephant galloping across a field of tin cans, and was almost surprised when gazelle-like Asia didn't dart away in surprise. In fact, she didn't even tear her eyes away from the painting she was studying. Instead, she just waited a moment for Will to settle beside her. "There's something about this one," she said at last.

Will took in the image—an old-fashioned painting done in classical style. It was of a bird with a woman's head. She was diving toward a ship, talons extended, a look of rage twisted across her beautiful features. Her hair was wild, and the men on the deck of the ship cowered in fear before her. Will checked the information plate beside the painting. *Siren,* it read. *MacDougal, Joan. American. 1851–1927.* "I thought sirens were mermaids," Will said.

Asia cocked her head. "Some say fish, some say birds."

"Tomato, tomahto," Will joked.

Asia looked at him, a smile playing at the edges of her lips. Will wasn't sure if Asia thought his joke was amusing . . . or if she thought Will was an idiot. *Say something smart,* he told himself. "I like the way this wing is painted here." He gestured to the extended wing, where every feather was rendered with precision.

Asia digested this in silence. She continued to study the painting. "I like the darkening sky," she said at last. "The cliffs."

Will peered closely at the cliffs in the background. The image of the bird-woman had grabbed his attention so thoroughly that he hadn't really noticed them. But there were indeed gray-white cliffs in the distance. And, perched atop the cliffs and executed in minute detail, were three more bird-women calmly watching the scene. Beneath their talons were several skulls. One was not quite picked clean.

Will felt his hands go cold.

"Exactly," Asia said, watching his face.

"Have you seen the rest of the exhibit?" Will asked suddenly. He wanted to get away from that picture.

Asia seemed to understand his feelings. She moved on, taking an unhurried stroll around the gallery. Will feigned interest in a sculpture of a conch shell that was made of a thousand smaller shells, but really he was watching Asia. There was something about that girl he couldn't figure out. The way she walked—with such confidence, but no arrogance—stood out in this small town. Will remembered the glance she had given him through the rain-spattered windshield. It had held him in place, the way her voice had the other day. It was better to stand back, watch her from a distance. Asia almost seemed like a visitor from another planet. Most of the paintings and sculptures garnered only a quick glance from Asia. One wall-sized photograph of several campy, smiling mermaids in pink wigs actually got a laugh. Finally she joined Will at the sculpture. She studied the smaller shells and the place where they joined together to swirl into one larger shell.

"The interconnection of the many and the one," Asia said at last.

"Really?" Will cocked his head. "Because this thing just makes me want some fried clams."

Asia laughed. It was a pretty sound, like silver bells.

"Hey, listen—do you—do you want to go get something to eat?" Will asked. "Like, some fried clams?"

Asia looked surprised, as if that was the last thing she had expected him to ask. Her voice was slow, like dragging feet, but she said, "All right. Yes."

They stepped out into the bright sunshine, and Will pointed to the left. "There's a really good place down near the water."

"Dave's?" Asia asked.

Will was surprised. Somehow he hadn't expected Asia to know about the divey little clam shack haunted by locals. "Yeah."

They fell into step in silence as they moved up the street. After two blocks, the rich, heady scent of fried food wafted over them. They ordered at the counter, then took their food to a picnic table on an open porch. The waves crashed on nearby rocks, and a friendly breeze blew as they arranged the red plastic baskets full of fried clams and french fries. Across the table from him, Asia seemed out of place in the mundane scene. For a moment he wondered what he was doing, bringing her here. But Asia smiled as she looked out at the sea. She didn't seem uncomfortable at all.

Will dipped a fry into a small plastic tub of creamy tartar sauce. "So—how'd you end up working at Bella's?"

Asia took a moment before answering, as if she was considering her words. "I wanted a job where I could get to know people," she said finally.

"There are a lot of shops where you could have done that," Will pointed out. "Or you could have been a camp counselor."

"I wasn't interested in those people," Asia said.

"You were interested in the people at Bella's?"

Asia smiled. "You're very inquisitive."

"Not usually," Will admitted. He fought the urge to ask her about walking into the sea. It wasn't the moment—not yet.

"I enjoy talking to people," Asia said. "Is that so strange?"

He wanted to tell her that she didn't act like someone who enjoyed talking to people. She wasn't really acting like she wanted to talk to him, for example. But that would be obnoxious, he knew, so he stayed silent.

Two high school girls that Will vaguely knew sat down at a table nearby. They stared at Asia with barely disguised contempt. Will had seen girls give Gretchen that look sometimes, too. "Most people have horrible personalities," Will said.

Asia nibbled a clam and nodded. "Many people," she corrected. "Not most."

"Enough," Will said. "I see it at our farm stand all the time. People cut in line, they're rude to each other, they talk on their cell phones and ignore whoever's behind the counter. It drives me nuts."

"Well do I know it."

"Well do I know it," Will repeated.

Asia's green eyes lingered on his, reading the amusement on his face. "Was that strangely put?"

"Strangely put?" Will laughed.

"What's so funny?" Asia asked.

"I don't know . . . sometimes some of what you say sounds kind of old-fashioned."

Asia popped a clam into her mouth and thought it over. "I should watch more TV, I guess."

"No, no—it's cool. I like it."

"I'm glad you approve."

"There you go again."

Asia smiled at him, and his heart tripped a little. "So tell me more about you," Will said.

"What would you like to know?"

Everything, he wanted to say. But, somehow, he didn't dare. This moment, with the air in his face and the strange, beautiful girl—it was so dreamlike that he was almost afraid to assert himself too much. He didn't want to wake up. "Tell me anything."

Asia shrugged.

"Okay . . . tell me about your family."

Asia placed her hands on the countertop. Her long white fingers spread like tentacles, then were still. She looked at Will, and suddenly he felt as if he had slipped down a well. He was disoriented, as if he were falling . . . falling . . .

"I had a sister," Asia said at last. Her eyes turned down to the table.

And that was all.

"I'm sorry."

"Thank you."

Silence.

"How did she die?"

Green eyes snapped up, met Will's face. "In a fire."

Will winced. He didn't say that he was sorry again, although he wanted to. It was hard to say the words, but he forced them out: "I had a brother."

"Yes," Asia told him. "I know."

He felt as if he had been stabbed in the heart—cold shock, disorienting pain. "You know?"

"Gretchen told me."

"Ah." Will looked to the window that opened onto the street. Someone was singing beneath a tree by the curbside. The kid had stringy hair and a tall, awkward body, and he was singing a sad song—something about the sea. It was Kirk Worstler.

The song seemed to be an old sailor's song, but it wasn't one that Will knew:

> *There's no sign of canvas upon the*
> *blue waves;*
> *You'll never return home to me.*
> *For the waves beat the shore*
> *Like a knock at the door,*
> *And all things return to the sea.*

The song floated over them. Kirk had a surprisingly beautiful tenor voice.

"There's something about losing a sibling, I think . . . ," Will said at last.

"It haunts you," Asia said.

Haunts. Yes, that was the word. Will felt haunted.

The hardest thing for Will to accept was that Tim would never be anything else—never anything else but dead. It didn't comfort Will to think of him in heaven, waiting for all of his loved ones to die and join him. And it didn't comfort him to think that God had a plan. If God had a plan, surely it wasn't a plan to kill off an eighteen-year-old right after his first year of college, to tear him from his mother before his life had even begun. What kind of crappy plan was that? These things that people said to Will—"Everything happens for a purpose," "He's with your grandfather now," "It's God's will"—all of these murmurings were just words to Will. He understood that people wanted to comfort him. But the words were just pitiful attempts to distract him from the fact that Tim was gone, and that nothing in Will's life—not a wife, not a career, not children—would ever be Tim. People spoke to him of the circle of life. *But life isn't a circle,* Will thought. *It's a straight line leading in one direction—like a gang-plank.*

The only people who really bothered Will were the "cherish the memories" people. They kept insisting that Will should be thankful for the time that he and his brother had shared. They said that Will should always remember the good times and be on the look-out for signs of Tim everywhere. But Will didn't want to cherish the memories. Will didn't miss the idea of Tim—he missed Tim. The flesh-and-blood brother who had once busted Will's nose, and who had blamed Will when he broke a window in the potato barn, and who had cried so hard at the end of *Charlotte's Web* that he threw up.

So it was a relief, sort of, to find someone who really knew how he was feeling. *It haunts you.* "People keep telling me that I'll get over it, but—"

"You never get over it." Asia's voice was a hatchet falling—sharp, fatal.

"No?"

"Never." Asia's eyes burned.

At the nearby table, one of the girls leaned over to whisper to the other. They both laughed, casting narrow-eyed glances at Asia. He thought about how stupid it was to envy people you didn't even know. Sure, Asia was beautiful. But Will was certain that Asia would trade that beauty in a heartbeat to have her sister back. Those girls saw only the outside. They couldn't possibly guess the reality.

It haunts you. You never get over it.

"That's what I thought," Will said at last.

Chapter Six

From the Walfang Gazette
Mystery at the Miller

A mystery donor dropped a four-hundred-year-old gold doubloon in the donation box at the Miller Gallery sometime last week.

"I came across it when I emptied the box," said Marjorie Willstack, a gallery volunteer. "At first I thought it was a bottlecap. When I realized what it was, I nearly died of shock."

Jacob Worthington of Worthington's Fine Antiques, who specializes in rare, collectible coins, estimated that the doubloon could be worth as much as $6,000. "It certainly doesn't seem like the kind of thing someone would place in the box as a mistake," he said. "It's not the sort of object one would carry in a change purse."

The Miller is grateful for the gift, but asks that the donor come forward. . . .

Will ran his fingers over the recorder. He sat on his bed with legs crossed, the mussed covers pushed back around him. Guernsey was beside him, her warm chin resting on his knee.

Ever since Will had taken the flute to the antiques store, it had occupied a chunk of his mind. Why hadn't he ever heard Tim play it? Why would his brother have an ancient recorder, anyway? Why not just a regular flute? Where had it come from? Had Tim found it, or had someone given it to him?

The night air outside was still, cut only by the sound of crickets.

He looked at the smooth bone carefully, wondering what kind of animal it had come from. The recorder was the length of his forearm, so it must have come from something large. A deer, perhaps. Or a sheep.

Will tried to recall the tune of the song Kirk had been singing earlier, but it was hopeless. Tim's musical gift had passed over Will completely. Between Gretchen—who had a beautiful singing voice—and Tim's guitar and perfect vocal pitch, Will figured that he should have picked up some talent by osmosis. But he hadn't. Will had always liked it when Tim and Gretchen sang together. Sometimes Tim would play the guitar, and sometimes Johnny. Gretchen could hold down the melody while Tim carved out the low harmony. Will had always been tone-deaf, even before the accident that stole the hearing from his right ear, and the music had sounded like magic to him. It seemed greater than sound; it was a fabric Gretchen and Tim were weaving together. But it was pleasure mixed with pain. For even though Tim was his brother, not Gretchen's, and Gretchen was his friend, not Tim's, when they sang together Will felt the tender pain of exclusion. He knew they didn't mean to make him feel that way. It was as if they had lost themselves so completely in the music that Will had ceased to exist for them.

He was secretly glad that Gretchen never wanted to sing in public. He was relieved that she wouldn't join Tim's band. Will didn't want the world to hear them together. He knew what they would say. Gretchen with her wild beauty and Tim with the chiseled features of a movie star—everyone would think they were a couple. And even if they weren't, Will would feel like a child watching his parents drive away, without waving, in the family sedan.

Will placed his lips at the edge of the flute and blew a note. It emerged uneven, but Will was surprised at how sweet it sounded.

"I know, I know, I'm not the brilliant musician," Will said as Guernsey's low growl rumbled against his knee. He stroked her soft ears, black flecked with white—evidence of her age—and she nosed his fingers.

Will blew another note, placing his fingers over the holes. He had played the recorder in second-grade music class, but the cheap plastic flutes had sounded flat even in the best hands. This flute, by contrast, sounded crisp and silvery even beneath his clumsy fingers. He didn't know much about music, though, so he didn't know a tune to play. "Mary Had a Little Lamb," maybe, but that didn't seem like the right kind of song for this instrument. It needed something melancholy, or at least pensive.

As if in answer, a single note came from the open window. Guernsey leaped up, barking madly, making the bed groan and creak beneath her feet.

"Hey, hey, it's just an echo," Will said, patting Guernsey's side with a hearty *thunk thunk thunk*. She settled down to a low growl, then hopped off the bed. "You're leaving? You sure?" Will asked as Guernsey looked up at the door expectantly. He got up to let her out, and she trotted stiffly down the hall and down the stairs.

Will looked down at the flute, wondering where Asia had found hers. She had said it was a gift—yet she had sold it. It was strange how thoughts of Asia seemed to sneak up on him. Not in the same way that thoughts of Tim blindsided him. It was more as if thoughts of Asia nibbled at the edges of his mind like the minnows that tickled his leg when he stepped into the bay. Often he wasn't even conscious that he was thinking of her *again*. What had she meant when she said she had no family? Where did she come from? Why didn't he ever see her with anyone—didn't she have friends? What was it about her that seemed to fill his mind with fog? Was it her speech pattern? Her beauty? Or something else that he couldn't put his finger on?

Will placed the flute at the back of his bottom drawer and slid it closed. He crossed back to his bed and looked out the window.

He wished he could talk to Tim. It was strange to have your brother, your best friend, disappear overnight. *We always shared everything. Right up to the end.*

The sand lay spread before her like a vast ocean, and—like the ocean—it felt cool on her feet as she trudged onward. The sun beat down, but it wasn't hot. A cool wind blew, setting her teeth on edge, making her body rigid with cold. Gretchen kept moving, hoping to get warm.

She had to get to the lake.

She knew it was there, although she couldn't see it. The sand sloped slightly upward, and her muscles ached as she trudged on. The sand was dewy on her bare feet.

She did not ask herself why she was there. She knew. She had to get to the lake.

The breeze blew again, and this time it carried a gentle strain. It wasn't quite a song—more like a tone. A single note. Sweet and clear as the jingle of a silver bell on a crisp winter night. It carried her forward, her feet moving more quickly now.

She hurried toward the top of the ridge, but it was farther than she'd thought. Her breath thickened in her throat as she increased her pace. She could see the light fog from her mouth, like a dragon's snore, hanging on the air.

Another note joined the first, and this was like a golden bell. Warm and sweet, thick as honey. She could almost taste the music. She wanted to gobble it up.

She paused.

She had reached the height. There, below her, lay a glassy sea. And now she was running, running toward the water. She felt like a rock tumbling forward, the momentum taking over. The music grew louder, and more notes joined the first until it was a symphony of tones. All of them unique as they wove together to form a single strand.

Her toe touched the water's edge, and she hesitated, stopping to look in the smooth surface. She could tell by the midnight blue of the water that the shore was like a precipice. After only a few inches, there was a sheer drop. In the water, she could see herself, her blue eyes, her long blond hair falling forward so that the tips touched the water.

And beyond the surface, in the deep, there was a flame.

She bent closer to see. It flickered, and Gretchen realized that another flame twinkled near the first. And another. Soon the flames were a night sky of stars. She looked overhead to see their mirror image.

But the sun shone high in the sky.

Gretchen looked down into the water. Two of the stars seemed to burn more brightly than the others. Their light glowed blue, like the hottest stars, then green. Suddenly they seemed like a pair of eyes.

As they glowed brighter still, Gretchen saw a face, pale and smooth. Then, around the face, tendrils of hair floated like seaweed.

Something moved, as if the face was trying to whisper something to her. The music caressed her with its own breeze. She leaned closer—and a hand grabbed her hair.

Her shriek suffocated as the hand pulled her face into the water. She kicked and fought, but it was no use. The thing was stronger. And now she could see that the flames were eyes, and they blazed with a dangerous fire, a fierce hate. The jaws snapped at her with dagger teeth. "Gretchen!" it snarled, and the silver bells turned to iron, ringing her chest with an alarm.

She choked and sputtered; she couldn't breathe. She clawed at the creature, but it held her and would not let go. . . .

"Gretchen!"

With a final effort, she kicked at the creature, and all at once it opened its grip. The thing cried out with a familiar voice, and when Gretchen looked up, she saw that it was dark as night outside.

Rocks bit into her hands; her knees throbbed where the flesh had been torn away. She was on her knees at the edge of the bluff. She barely had time to register that she had been sleepwalking again when something moved.

"Gretchen!" shouted a voice. Will's voice.

The thing moved again, and Gretchen realized that it was his hand. It was gripping the earth with white knuckles. He had fallen over the edge of the bluff and was clinging to the rocks for dear life.

He must have been trying to stop me from going over, Gretchen realized. *I was sleepwalking again.* "Will!" Gretchen crawled forward, but she was too slow. His hand slipped, then disappeared. "Will!"

Gretchen scrambled to the edge and looked over. But all she saw was a deep blackness. And the only noise was the crashing of the waves on the rocks below.

Will came to with a sudden jerk, a spasm in his neck. "Ow."

"Shh."

Finger to the lips. Green eyes. Long dark hair spilling forward, brushing his chest lightly.

"Where—?" Will looked around. He heard the soft crash of the sea as he struggled to sit upright. All of his limbs seemed to be in working order, but his mind—that was another matter. *What is this stuff I'm lying on?* he wondered, running his hands on the softness. It wasn't rocks, which was what he had been expecting. It took him a moment to realize it was sand.

"You fell," Asia told him.

Will looked at her, wondering dimly what she was doing there. "I know." Yes, he remembered.

Will remembered exactly what happened.

From his second-story window, he had seen a figure in white slipping through the darkness. It was Gretchen. Although the night was dark, Will could see her clearly, as if she were illuminated with her own inner fire. Ghostlike, Gretchen made her way through the trees and headed toward the bluff.

"Damn," Will cursed under his breath, and yanked on his jeans. He shoved his feet into his sneakers and raced out the back door without tying the laces. The screen door banged behind him as he loped toward the willows.

For a moment he couldn't see her. Then—there, between the trunks—a flash of white. "Gretchen!" he shouted, plunging into the darkness after her.

Twice before he'd caught her sleepwalking. Once, when they were seven years old, Will had seen her on the porch, and he snuck out of the house to join her. Her eyes were open, and she spoke to him. But it was in a strange voice, with words he didn't understand.

It took him a while to realize that she wasn't awake, and then he was frightened. He'd heard that you could kill someone if you woke them while they were sleepwalking, and he was still young enough to believe it. He didn't dare shout for help, and he didn't dare to leave her. So they sat there for over two hours, until Will's father went to check on him and realized that he wasn't in bed. He found Will and Gretchen on Gretchen's porch swing. Gretchen had fallen fully asleep, her head in a wide-eyed Will's lap.

The next time was four years later. Will had heard a noise downstairs, so he grabbed his baseball bat and crept into the kitchen. There was Gretchen. She was bathed in the warm light of the fridge as she stood before its open door, staring blankly at the bags of turnips, the wilting greens, the chicken thighs, the iced tea, the half-empty jar of mayonnaise, the bottle of chocolate syrup. Will took her hand and gently closed the fridge. Then he led her out the door, down the steps. His feet were slippery with dew as he led her across the lawn to her house, where a frantic Johnny had just realized she was missing.

These were Will's thoughts as he stumbled after Gretchen in the dark. He was afraid that she might hurt herself. If she reached the bluff, she could fall. . . .

He doubled his pace. A branch whipped across his cheek, a rock found its way into his shoe, but he didn't stop.

In a moment he was beyond the trees and could see her, moving quickly across the wide sweep of grass that led to the bluff. The distant roar of the ocean grew nearer, more dangerous.

She paused for a moment, looked up at the gibbous moon with her unseeing eyes.

"Gretchen!"

She darted forward, her long legs racing toward the precipice. Will's breath was thick and heavy in his throat. The long muscles in his thighs burned as he tore up the incline. She was five steps from the edge. Three. Two.

"Gretchen!" Will shouted, reaching for her. A fistful of fabric, and he yanked her back. She raked her nails across his face and let out an unearthly scream. She hit at his throat, choking him. He struggled for breath, but he wouldn't let go.

Gretchen gave a sudden, violent kick. Will cried out as he fell to his knees. "Wake up!" he cried as she kicked again.

His knee slipped as blows rained down on him—he was shocked at her strength. His leg skidded over the edge of the bluff, his foot straining for purchase against gravel and rock. Will reached for the ground with his hands, but he grasped only earth. He reached for her leg, but one last, terrible kick sent him reeling backward. "Gretchen!" he cried as his fingers struggled to keep their grip on the gravel.

He couldn't see the waves below, but he could hear them. He knew the rocks well. Mountainous boulders of slick red granite. Jagged as shark teeth, and as unforgiving.

His arms ached with strain as he struggled to pull

himself upward. But the ground crumbled beneath his fingers, and in a sickening plunge, he fell back into thin air. A searing flash against the back of his head, and then even the stars went black. . . .

And now, green eyes. Asia. Her face was clear in the light of the fattening moon.

"What are—? How did you—?" He sat up, then stood uncertainly, testing the pain in his body. He squeezed his eyes shut. Aches. Soreness. But nothing broken. He could feel a knot forming—he must have hit the back of his head when he went over the edge. But he wasn't at the foot of the rocks. He was on the sand at the base of the bluff, a hundred feet away. It was as if a breeze had blown in and carried him to safety. He opened his eyes. "What happened?"

No answer.

He turned, and found himself alone. Asia had simply disappeared.

Will fought the feeling of unreality that was creeping over him like an army of ants. *Maybe I was sleepwalking. Maybe I am—*

"Will!" someone shrieked. "Will!"

It was Gretchen's voice.

"Here!" he called.

"Will? Will?" A figure in white tore down the bluff. "Oh my God!" In a moment, Gretchen reached him, wrapped him in a hug. "Oh my God." She sobbed against his bare chest, and suddenly Will's teeth began to chatter in the cold night air. He was shivering, desperately cold, but relief made his joints feel fluid and loose.

"It's okay." Will patted her hair awkwardly. "I'm okay."

"I thought you were—"

"I'm not."

"But you—" She looked back at the bluff. Put a hand to her forehead. "I was dreaming."

"I know."

"What happened?"

Will shook his head. "No clue."

"But you were up there." She gestured toward the bluff. Then her face crumpled in confusion. "Weren't you?"

"I think so."

Gretchen slipped her slender fingers into his, intertwining them like bean vines. "Are we both going crazy?" she whispered.

Will couldn't quite make himself say no. "I don't know," he said instead.

"Great," Will said bitterly as they neared his house. It was lit up, as if they had turned every light on in the place so they could look for him in the shadows—behind the couch, in the corners of the closet. His mother was probably tearing the house apart to try to find him. He could practically hear her wearing the floorboards smooth with her pacing.

"I'll go in with you," Gretchen offered.

"You don't have to," Will told her.

Gretchen squeezed his hand as if she couldn't let it go, and Will realized that she was still shaking. The trembling had passed through his body like an earthquake, leaving him exhausted and dazed. He imagined the rubble of fallen buildings, windows shattered, bricks and rocks and scattered papers blowing down a deserted street. That was how he felt: wasted.

Gretchen, on the other hand, looked down at him with wide eyes, pupils dilated. Her hand felt hot—she was almost burning him with the intensity of her grip—and Will realized that she was frightened. Terrified. For her, the earthquake was still happening.

"Come on," he said.

Guernsey was the first to hear their footfall on the step at the side door, and she came *clack-clack-clacking* across the linoleum to greet them, tail wagging. Her movements were slow and stiff with age, and she hadn't quite reached them when Mrs. Archer darted in from the next room, face pale, eyes wide.

"Will!" Her voice was a strangled scream as she flung the screen door wide, shoving the dog aside.

"I'm all right, Mom, I'm—"

Pain tore across his face as she slapped him, hard.

Nobody moved.

"How could you do that to me?" she whispered. Tears gathered at the rims of her eyes, pooled, then spilled down onto the slack of her hollow cheeks. She was wearing her ugly flowered nightgown—the one with the collar that buttoned up to her neck—and, over that, a battered yellow terrycloth bathrobe. She looked ancient and tired.

Guernsey sat down, ears back, and stared up at

Mrs. Archer, watching her carefully. "Oh, God, Will." She grabbed him and pulled him into a hug. "Don't do that," she whispered. "Don't do that."

The clock on the wall ticked on, and a shadow appeared in the kitchen doorway. It was Will's father. He looked from Will to Gretchen, who was still clinging to Will's arm like a frightened little girl. "Where you kids been?" he asked.

Mrs. Archer seemed to notice Gretchen for the first time. A blush bloomed across her face and she dried her eyes quickly.

Will was still too angry to say anything, but Gretchen spoke up. "I was sleepwalking again. Will saw me. He—" She looked up at Will, gave his hand another squeeze. "I was headed for the bluff. I got all the way to the edge."

Mrs. Archer gasped and reached for Gretchen's hand. "Good God, girl."

"Will saw me from his window. He came after me," Gretchen said. She shivered.

Mrs. Archer's eyes lit on her son, and she seemed to take in the bloody scratch on his face.

Mr. Archer nodded. "I thought it might be something like that. Don't just stand there, Evelyn, get the girl some tea."

"No, that's all right," Gretchen said, but Mrs. Archer had already hurried over to the stove and was filling up the kettle.

Mr. Archer pulled out a chair, and Gretchen sank into it gratefully. Guernsey hobbled over and plopped at Gretchen's feet. Will continued to stand. He folded his arms across his chest, suddenly aware that he was half naked. His chest and arms were lightly muscled and tan from farm work. It was strange how he never felt awkward with his shirt off while he was outside in the summertime, but here, in the closeness of the kitchen with his parents and Gretchen, he felt exposed.

"Has this been happening a lot?" Will asked.

"More lately," Gretchen admitted.

"You need to take some warm milk before bed," Mrs. Archer said as she dropped a teabag into a white mug and filled it with steaming water. "Or chamomile. The best tea for calming the mind." She placed the mug on the table in front of Gretchen.

"I've tried," Gretchen told her. "I've tried everything—yoga, meditation, tea, whatever. Nothing works. Not even sleeping pills." She shook her head, then blew lightly on the tea. But she didn't pick it up.

"Maybe you should lock yourself in your room," Will suggested.

Gretchen looked up at him, hurt registering on her face, and Will winced. His words had sounded sarcastic, although he hadn't meant them to.

"I'm sorry," Gretchen said weakly.

"I didn't mean—"

"Will, you're a godawful mess," Mr. Archer put in. "Why don't you go wash that crust off your face and put on something that isn't covered in dirt?"

Will nodded, happy to have an excuse to disappear for a moment. "Yeah. I'll do that."

* * *

Mr. Archer retreated to the living room as Will's footsteps shuffled up the stairs. For a moment, the only sound in the kitchen was Guernsey's gentle snoring. Then a creak and a sigh as Mrs. Archer slid into the chair across from Gretchen. She sipped her tea with a slurp, swallowing loudly.

"I'm glad you're all right," Mrs. Archer said into her tea.

"Thanks to Will," Gretchen said.

Mrs. Archer looked up. "Yes." She cleared her throat. "Well." She frowned, shrugged. "I just don't know what I'd do if anything happened to you. I think of you like a daughter, you know."

Gretchen felt her eyebrows shoot up in surprise. *Where is that coming from?* Will's mother wasn't usually so open with her feelings.

Mrs. Archer placed her hand over Gretchen's. Then she leaned so far forward that Gretchen could feel her breath. She smelled the mint of her toothpaste, the sweetness of the chamomile. "I know about Tim," Mrs. Archer whispered fiercely. "I know how much he—"

Gretchen drew her hand away in shock, but at that moment Will came bounding down the stairs in a pair of shorts and a T-shirt. He had washed the blood off his face, revealing only a small scratch on his left cheek. Smaller than the scar on the other side, but symmetrical. Gretchen's head swam with relief. She didn't want to discuss Tim. Not now.

Mrs. Archer stood up and crossed to the sink, where she placed her mug carefully. "Will, you should take Gretchen home," she said, her back turned to her son.

"You ready?" Will asked Gretchen.

"Sure." She handed the mug to Mrs. Archer, who accepted it like a token. "Thanks for the tea."

Mrs. Archer nodded, her piercing gaze strangely unmatched to Gretchen's light words.

Will didn't notice, though. He just held open the door for Gretchen and let her walk through it.

All the way across the lawn to her dark house, Gretchen couldn't help wondering what Mrs. Archer had been about to say. She knew about Tim. But what exactly had he told her? Not the whole story. That was impossible.

The day Tim died, he had made a confession to Gretchen. She had gone for a walk at the edge of the bay. He had seen her from his bedroom window, and had joined her. He'd looked serious and miserable. And then he told her that he loved her.

"Tim," she'd started, but he put a finger to her lips.

"I know," Tim said, staring down at her with his intense brown eyes. "It's Will, isn't it?"

She'd felt the tears spill over the rims of her eyes, but she couldn't answer.

"Does he know?" Tim asked.

Gretchen shook her head.

Tim pulled her into a hug, and he didn't seem to mind the tears on his shirt, or the fact that Gretchen's nose was dripping. "You should tell him," he whispered into her hair.

But she couldn't tell him. She couldn't risk it. Whether or not he felt the same way, the moment she said something, things between them would never be the same. Gretchen wasn't ready for that. And then Tim had died, and Gretchen had started to doubt that she'd ever be able to tell Will the truth.

"Do you want me to go inside with you?" Will asked when they reached her door. It was unlocked, as usual. Nobody locked their doors around here.

"I'll be fine," Gretchen told him. She wanted to give him a hug but suddenly felt too fragile. "Good night."

"Sleep well," Will told her. "Hope the chamomile works."

Gretchen smiled weakly, then turned and walked into the dark hall. Will started back toward his house. Gretchen looked back to her front door, thinking about her dream, about how Will had fallen over the edge yet landed down the beach . . . Her mind churned and buzzed with questions that had no answers.

Chapter Seven

Women of the Rocks (Traditional)

The women, the women, they call you to sea
With skin alabaster and lips of ruby,
With voices of angels as soft as a sigh,
And touches like fire that call you to die.

Gretchen dipped a toe into the crystalline water. "It's warm," she said, surprised.

"Heated," Jason said as he stripped off his navy T-shirt. Three quick steps and he leaped out over the water, pulling his legs into a cannonball.

Gretchen screeched as the splash sent drops spewing all over her. "You jerk!" she cried playfully as Jason broke the surface and shook his head, sending out a shower like a lawn sprinkler.

A gardener looked up from the hedge he was clipping, then quickly turned back to his work. He was Filipino, one of three workers busily weeding, mulching, and trimming the property. Jason's mother had rented a different house this year, and the yard was pristine and very private. An ancient apple tree grew in the center of the yard, partially shading a collection of green and white hostas. Everything was surrounded by towering boxwoods and trimmed with periwinkle-blue hydrangeas. The brick-rimmed pool was near the house, and there was a pretty little ironwork cafe table with a market umbrella and four chairs. Gretchen imagined taking a morning swim in the pool, then drinking an espresso by the water. She didn't usually like pools, but the lush garden surrounding this one made it seem like a natural part of the landscape, almost like a lake.

"Coming in?" Jason asked.

Gretchen pulled off her blue sundress and laid it across one of the iron chairs. She felt Jason's eyes linger on her body, hesitating only momentarily at the scratches on her knees, as she stepped cautiously into the pool. Once Gretchen reached the bottom stair, she dove forward and swam up to Jason. "Mmm," she said as she surfaced. The just-cool water slicked back her hair and left her feeling refreshed, washing away the exhaustion she'd been carrying from the night before. Both the sleepwalking and dealing with her father's overwrought reaction when he saw her walk in through the front door had drained her. "That feels good."

Jason watched her lips hungrily. He stepped forward, pressing his body against hers. His skin was smooth, slippery in the water. He kissed her, his lips warm and sweet.

Her mind whirled back to last summer, to the moment when they met. Gretchen had gone to a gallery to check out a retrospective of one of her favorite artists. The paintings were Pollock-like drips and splashes, but in gentler tones that suggested ripples and waves. She had talked Johnny into taking her to the opening, which was crowded with the tanned and the thin.

Most of the sparkling crowd seemed to be more interested in talking to each other than in the art. Gretchen kept trying to look at the paintings, only to find herself being elbowed aside by someone reaching for an hors d'oeuvre or a glass of red wine. She finally found a far corner and managed to spend three uninterrupted minutes inspecting a miniature triptych.

"Thanks, Dad," Gretchen said as Johnny wordlessly handed her a Coke.

He gave her a *do we have to stay much longer?* smile, and she kissed him on the cheek. "I just want to look at a few more paintings," she told him.

"Take your time," Johnny told her before disappearing into the social swirl.

"Isn't he a little old for you?" A platinum-haired hunk had appeared at her elbow. There was a smirk in his voice, but Jason's face was impassive, as if there wasn't an answer that could possibly surprise him.

"That's my dad," Gretchen told him.

Jason nodded. He looked at the painting. "What do you think of this?"

"I think it's beautiful."

"I hate beautiful art," Jason said.

"What's wrong with beauty?" Gretchen shot back.

"It just doesn't do anything for me."

"I don't believe you."

Jason smirked. "You're right." His eyes skimmed her body, and she felt her face burn.

Gretchen found herself wondering why she was talking to this person. He was forward and she wasn't sure she liked it.

"I'm Jason," he said, as if he'd read her thoughts.

"Gretchen."

"You're an artist." Not a question.

"What makes you say that?"

"Because you're the only one here who's looking at the art. Everyone else is here to be seen. You'd think that they were the ones hanging on the walls."

"Why are you here?"

"This is my mother's gallery," he said. "I don't want to hurt her feelings by not coming to her opening." His voice was gentle when he said it, without the slightest trace of a smirk.

"You and your mom are close?" Gretchen asked.

"I live with my dad most of the time, but yeah, I'm closer to my mom."

And that was when Gretchen had found herself confiding to Jason that she was closer to her dad—that her mom lived far away and never contacted them. They'd connected. And he was handsome. There was no doubt about that.

Now, in the pool, she melted against him, and his hand traveled up her side. A fingertip slipped beneath her bikini top, and she pulled away. "Jason," she warned.

"What?" He pulled her closer, but she struggled against him.

"The gardeners."

Jason looked up as if he hadn't even realized that there were other people in the yard. They were at the other end of the wide green lawn, one up on a tall ladder with electric shears. Jason twirled his fingers into the ropes of her hair. "They don't care." His voice was a husky whisper.

"*I* care." Gretchen felt herself blushing.

Jason narrowed his eyes. Then he gave her hair a yank. It was too hard to be playful, but he splashed away like a grinning otter. "Whatever." Again his tone was nonchalant, but he sent a giant splash at her face, then headed for the side of the pool.

"Where are you going?" Gretchen asked as Jason hauled himself out of the pool.

"I need some iced tea," he called without looking over his shoulder. "I'll be back."

Gretchen stood at the center of the pool, feeling idiotic. *Why did I have to ruin the mood?* she wondered. Then again, it was Jason who was being a jerk. *So why am I feeling so bad?* Every now and then, an elbow of the rage that Jason kept clamped down would poke out, knocking at those nearby. She had forgotten how much it had bothered her last summer, how often it had left her confused and sometimes frightened. And it was usually over something small. A glass of soda with too much ice. Obnoxious air-conditioning. People on cell phones. *Is it so wrong to feel weird about making out in front of strangers? Is that really something to get furious over?*

He hadn't even asked if she wanted some iced tea.

"I'd like the mahi mahi with the mango-avocado infusion." Angus grinned at Gretchen as he plopped onto the red vinyl bar stool at the counter. "And a glass of rosemary tea."

"I think we're out of that. How about some coffee that's strong enough to fry your face?"

"Even better. I'll take one of those pumpkin muffins, too."

Gretchen poured a mug and set it down on the counter before him. She snapped a piece of wax paper from the box and lifted the glass cover over the muffins. Gretchen looked them over carefully before placing one on a plate and carrying it to Angus.

Angus drummed his long fingers on the table. "I saw that," he said. "You gave me the biggest one." He waggled his eyebrows, then took a long swig from the coffee, and his eyes went round. "Whoa."

"I warned you."

"What's in this? Tobacco juice?"

Gretchen laughed. "Just coffee. It'll pick you up, that's for sure." She grabbed a handful of creamers, and when she turned back, she saw that Angus had flipped her sketchbook around to get a better look.

"That's nothing," she said, reaching for it.

He slapped her hand lightly and looked up at her with a frown. "I am *appreciating* art," he said primly.

Gretchen looked down at the counter. She felt the blush creeping up her neck. There was something about having people look at her work that always made her feel naked. When she looked up, she noticed that someone was watching her. Kirk Worstler had skulked into a corner booth earlier in the afternoon and had been sitting there—drinking a soda and staring in his creepy way—for nearly ninety minutes. Gretchen forced her eyes away from him.

"This is really amazing." Angus took another sip of coffee, wincing slightly. "The feathers alone . . ." He gestured to the drawing. It was a woman in profile, her arm reaching skyward. Most of her naked back was obscured by two enormous white wings. Long dark hair fluttered to the side, as if blown in a breeze. In the distance were tall cliffs and crashing waves. Rocks hulked at the bottom of the precipice, and the waves hurled themselves against them furiously, sending foam spewing toward the sky. "Where did you even come up with this?"

"I had this dream," Gretchen confessed.

"Beautiful."

Gretchen's blush deepened. "Thanks."

Angus turned it back toward her and broke off a piece of his muffin. "So, listen, what time do you get off work?"

"Three," Gretchen said. "Why?"

"I thought you might want to head over to the Commons with me tonight. It's the first night of Big Screen. The theme is Elvis," he added in a singsong.

"Oh, sure. Maybe Will wants to come, too." She reached into the pocket of her apron for her cell phone, but Angus put a gentle hand on her forearm.

"I thought it could just be the two of us this time," Angus said. His voice was heavy with meaning as Gretchen looked into his dark eyes.

Gretchen's heart stopped a moment. She'd never actually noticed before that Angus was handsome. Maybe he never *had* been handsome before. She'd always thought of him as lanky and awkward, but now she realized that he was simply tall. In fact, he was slim in a rather elegant way. He'd done something with his hair—the formerly shaggy mop was now tamed so that you could see his eyes and the dark lashes that framed them. There was a splash of boyish freckles across his tan face. And when he gave that impish smile—like the one he was giving her now—he was charming.

"It's *Jailhouse Rock*," Angus said.

"What?"

"The movie. It's a classic." Seeing her hesitation, he added, "Don't tell me that you don't like Elvis."

"I've never really listened—"

"Then we *have* to go!" Angus slapped the counter, and a couple of the other customers looked up.

Gretchen hesitated, squirming with discomfort. She really liked Angus, and she didn't want to hurt his feelings. Besides, part of her wanted to say yes. After all, the movie sounded like fun. She loved seeing films on the giant outdoor screen they set up at the Commons. You'd bring a blanket and a picnic and lie on the grass, cheering along with the crowd under the stars. But she knew that Angus could never be more to her than a friend. And he wasn't like Jason. Angus had a heart that could be broken.

The light at the glass door dimmed as a dark shape—Jason—yanked it open. He paused a moment, looking for her, his bulk blocking the light.

Angus followed her gaze, and his expression hardened. "Right," he said, unfolding himself from the stool like a pocketknife. He gave her a smile, but his face was set—a wax mask. "I guess you could never go for just a regular nice guy, right?"

"I don't know," Gretchen whispered, but Angus was already walking away.

Jason was oblivious to the cold glare Angus shot him in passing. Her boyfriend spotted Gretchen and stalked over.

"Hey, what's up?" he asked as he plopped onto Angus's still-warm stool. He glanced down at Gretchen's drawing, then shoved it aside without comment. "What are we doing tonight?"

We? It wasn't like Jason had ever asked her out or anything. Gretchen handed him a cup of coffee the way he liked it—loads of cream, two sugars. "Want to go see an Elvis movie on the Commons?"

A faint, slightly patronizing smile. "Are you serious?"

"Yeah. It sounds like fun."

Jason snorted. "No way." He set his mug on her notebook.

Her *open* notebook. The wet bottom settled across the carefully articulated wings.

The gasp was silent, but she felt it in her chest. She was frozen. She'd heard of archaeologists finding specimens perfectly preserved in ice, as if they'd been caught in a sudden ice age. That was how she felt—like a helpless mastodon that had stumbled onto the wrong glacier. And then, on the heels of the ice, came fire. Rage seared through Gretchen's body. Reaching out, she grabbed Jason's wrist.

"Ow—shit!" Jason yanked his arm back with such force that he stumbled backward off his stool. He held up his arm. His wrist was red, a small blister forming at the base of his palm.

Gretchen stared, her heart hammering. She felt something, like a butterfly wing against her cheek. When she looked up, she saw that Asia was watching her. Watching Jason.

"What the hell?" Jason demanded. "Is this because of your stupid drawing?" He took a threatening step toward Gretchen.

Before Gretchen could react, Asia moved forward. "Get out," she said.

Jason's jaw went rigid and his hand tightened into a fist.

Asia leaned toward him. "You can't move," she whispered softly, sweetly.

Jason's face twisted in rage. Gretchen was pressed against the steel sink, watching his muscles strain against an invisible barrier. "Let . . . go . . ." he snarled.

But Asia wasn't touching him.

Angel darted out from behind the grill. The customers fell silent, staring as Jason and Asia glared at each other.

"Let go!" Jason screeched. "I'll sue your ass!"

Asia laughed. It was a real laugh—not a mocking laugh—as if Jason had said something funny.

Jason lunged, stumblingly, as if he had been pushing against a door that suddenly gave way. Angel darted forward as Jason reached for Asia, and a piercing scream sounded from a corner booth. It was high and loud, and cut through the diner like a laser. It went on and on—much longer than a normal shriek. It was more like a siren or an alarm.

Everyone turned to look.

"Oh, God," Gretchen gasped. Kirk Worstler was standing on the table, screaming. His fists were clamped into his dark hair, his eyes fixed on Asia. Finally his voice died away. He took another breath and started screaming again.

"Jesus Christ, shut up!" Angel shouted. He scrambled toward Kirk, who jumped away, monkey-like. He leaped onto the back of the next booth, then to the floor. Angel reached for him, but Kirk ran toward the back and darted, still screaming, out the back door.

"Everyone in here is fucking crazy!" Jason shouted.

"You!" Angel stormed over to Jason and put a finger in his face. His voice dropped, and he snarled from beneath his moustache. "You get the hell out of here."

Jason slapped Angel's finger away. He turned to Asia. "This isn't over."

"I know," Asia told him.

Jason didn't even glance in Gretchen's direction before stalking out of Bella's.

For a moment everyone was silent. Then the chatter resumed at twice the usual volume. Asia turned and locked eyes with Gretchen for a moment. That was when Gretchen realized that she was trembling.

"Oh, Lord, honey!" Lisette hurried over to Gretchen. "Are you okay?"

"I'm—" Gretchen didn't know what to say. *Fine? Freaked out?*

Lisette didn't seem to need a full answer. She squeezed Gretchen's shoulder as Angel leaned across the counter and looked into her face. "That guy is never setting foot in here again," he announced.

"I'm sorry," Gretchen mumbled.

Angel narrowed his eyes. "For what? Living in a world filled with assholes?" He picked up Jason's still-full coffee mug and handed it to Lisette. She dumped the coffee down the drain, then tossed the cup into the other sink, the one Gretchen had been leaning against. The sink was half filled with soapy water, and when Lisette dropped the cup in, a few drops flew up and splashed her hand. She sucked in her breath, her face contorting in pain.

"You okay?" Angel asked.

"Yeah—that water is boiling hot." Lisette shook her fingers.

Angel scowled at her. "No more injuries today, okay? No more fights, no nothing. I want it nice and quiet." He turned to Asia, who was still standing nearby. "That goes for you, too."

Asia nodded, then turned quietly toward a table of customers.

"You take a fifteen-minute break," Angel commanded Gretchen. Then he stormed back toward his grill.

"My hand is feeling much better, thanks!" Lisette called after him. She rolled her eyes. "That guy could make you crazy."

She went back to her tables as Gretchen made her way to the bathroom. She flicked on the fluorescent light and splashed water onto her face. Once she had dried her face with a few scratchy brown paper towels, she looked at herself in the mirror, trying to understand what had just happened. She'd grabbed Jason's wrist. She hadn't meant to grab it so hard, but that angry red blister proved she had hurt him. And then, when he'd started toward her, Asia had stopped him somehow.

It's amazing how quickly things can get out of control, Gretchen thought. *How fast they can change.*

Things with Jason were over. She was shocked at how relieved she felt.

After a few minutes, someone knocked at the door. "Just a moment," Gretchen called. She arranged her hair and straightened her uniform.

And just like that, she thought as she reached for the doorknob, *life goes on.*

He felt like the world's worst spy, waiting for her to come out of the diner. Darkness had stolen silently over the town, but the restaurants were lit up. Even though it was only Thursday, they were packed with the rich and the beautiful. Will watched them as they sat at small cafe tables, lifting heavy silver forks to eat tiny portions of fresh bay scallops or salmon in a balsamic reduction. He was amazed at how clean they were, how fresh they seemed. Their clothes were perfectly pressed. Their skin was bronzed and smooth, their hair soft-looking and sweet-smelling. They ate slowly. They drank Coke or iced tea or sparkling water from green bottles.

Whenever Will's family went out, everyone drank tap water. His father considered anything else "money for nothing." Appetizers fell under the same category, as did desserts. He would pay for the main meal, and that, grudgingly. Will's father often complained that nothing was half as good as what Evelyn could make at home. Will usually agreed with him. He hated going out to eat—especially at nice restaurants. He hated being surrounded by all of those clean, clean people.

Around Will, the light from the restaurants fell soft and yellow onto the redbrick walkway. But across the street, the diner's neon sign glowed garishly pink and green, and the wide windows beamed bluish fluorescent light into the night air. The patrons, older and overfed, were backlit, and every feature was as visible as if Will had just pulled into a drive-in. But Will's eyes were trained on Asia.

The more he watched, the more amazed he was at her grace. Her movements were liquid, more beautiful than a dance. She balanced a white plate on her delicate hand. She turned her head, her neck arching gracefully. She maneuvered deftly around another waitress, as if she could sense others' quick change of direction. Beside her, the other waitresses looked clunky and awkward. As if they lived in different elements. Or different times. Like dinosaurs and birds—distantly related, bearing little family resemblance.

The dinner rush was over, and one by one the diners finished meals, wiped mouths, asked for checks. Will watched Asia clear tables, refill sugar shakers, sort silverware. He saw her chat with the cook and the other waitress—Gretchen had said her name was Lisette—as she swept the floor. Will saw her strawberry lips forming words, and hungered to know what they were. Will didn't care what she was saying. He wished he could catch each word from her mouth and preserve them in a jar, like fireflies.

Finally, finally, she pulled off her apron. She waved good-bye to the others. She headed out the door.

Will stood up, his legs stiff from sitting so long. He waited until she reached the end of the block, then hurried after her. "Hey," Will called when he saw her. "Hey!"

She didn't turn, so he jogged after her. He'd been waiting for her to finish her shift at the diner for the past forty-five minutes, and he wasn't about to miss his chance to talk to her.

She wove through the tourists, reminding Will of the many minnows he had tried to catch when he was young. They always darted through his fingers and disappeared into the murk of the creek that wound beside his house and fed into the bay.

Will increased his speed to a trot. "Hey!" he called as she rounded a corner.

This street wasn't so crowded. Leafy trees reached overhead in front of redbrick and wooden houses with overplanted window boxes. Toward the end of the street was a tiny restaurant, closed until the next day.

Will was running now. He was gaining on her—he was so close, he could almost touch her. He reached out—

And she turned to face him.

Momentum carried him forward; he almost ran into her. He planted his feet, but his body kept moving. He made a jerky little movement, like a puppet on a string or a dog yanked back by its owner.

Will planted his hands on his knees to catch his breath. "Hey," he said, looking up at her.

Asia just watched him with her cool green stare.

Finally Will straightened up. "So—" he began.

Asia lifted an eyebrow.

"So—what was that all about?" Will blurted out.

Asia blinked. Other than that, she was motionless.

"Last night? Hello?" He waved his hand in front of her face, as if to break her out of a trance. "I wake up and you're looking down at me. And I'm, like, fifty feet from where I'm supposed to be. Which is on some rocks, dead."

"Are you trying to say thank you?"

"So you *were* there!" He hadn't expected her to admit it so easily.

"Where, exactly?"

"Don't play dumb. You—you *did* something. You appeared from out of nowhere."

"How would that be humanly possible?"

"You tell me."

"It isn't." And she turned away.

"No," Will said, reaching for her arm. "Ouch!" He shook his hand—his fingers were numb.

She turned on him, fury in her eyes. "Be careful," she said in a low voice. There was something—a tone, a quality. Will didn't know. All he knew was that the world shifted suddenly. The anger that had been pulsing through his body like a piston drained away, leaving him loose-limbed and rubbery. He released his grip.

"I don't owe you anything," Asia told him in the same quiet voice. It was almost a song, but Will couldn't catch the melody.

He tried to repeat it. "You don't owe me anything."

"That's right."

She started away.

Will felt as if he had been submerged into water, warm as blood. He wanted to float away. He stumbled like a drunk toward a bench and sat down heavily. Asia watched him, then turned to glide away.

But wasn't there something he wanted to ask her?

What was it?

His tongue was thick, like it was covered in algae. It was an effort to move it. "What happened?"

Asia stopped, stiff as a board. Slowly, slowly, she turned to face him. "What?"

The fog was lifting. It was a superhuman effort, but Will rose to his feet. "How did I end up so far from where I fell?"

Asia was silent.

"What the hell is your deal, Asia? I swear to God I saw you walk right into the ocean during a hurricane, and now you seem to have flown up to some rocks to rescue me." Will's strength was coming back to him now. He pointed to the scar on his face. "Do you see this? I have no idea how I got this. People think I'm crazy. Even *I'm* starting to think I'm crazy. I don't need someone making me crazier. Now, how did I end up so far from where I fell?"

Asia's gaze held his, taut as a rope between them.

Will could have sworn that she didn't move her lips, but he heard her say, "You already know the answer."

He felt as if he had wandered into someone else's dream. He didn't know the boundaries. He couldn't wake up. But he wasn't frightened. Instead, his body felt heavy and warm. It was like drinking hot chocolate on a cold day, or curling up in bed with sad-eyed Guernsey lying against him.

"Am I just crazy?" he asked. He could almost see the words as they floated away from him, like butterflies.

Asia smiled and cocked her head. She looked up toward the dark sky, as if tracing the path of the words as they fluttered overhead.

She took a step toward him. Then another.

Her scent floated toward him. A faint sweetness, like lilies. And a light sea-air tang. He wanted to reach out and touch her—his body ached with the wanting. But he couldn't move. He was a seahorse, anchored to a single spot but swept by the current.

Asia stepped so close to him that her nose was almost touching his. She lifted her finger and touched his bottom lip, which tingled slightly under her fingertip.

Am I crazy? Will wondered.

This close, he could see how pale her skin was. A

delicate spiderweb of blue veins was visible along her forehead. And her eyes—they were the largest eyes he'd ever seen. As if she were some cave creature, able to see in the dark.

Am I?

"You aren't crazy, Will," she whispered.

Then she turned and walked away.

Will was left there, filled with fog. What was it about this girl? They'd had that moment of connection, and then she'd closed up as quickly as a clam. Will wondered if what he felt for her was a sort of passion. But it wasn't a passion that sharpened his senses. Instead, it clouded his mind and left him feeling drugged and sluggish. And it was different from lust. She was beautiful, and he found himself wanting to be near her, to touch her. But more than anything he simply wanted to understand her.

Yet the more he tried, the more she eluded him.

Slowly his faculties started to come back to him. He regained feeling in his hands, then his legs. He shook his head, then his whole body, the way Guernsey did when she stepped out of the creek. Then he took a step forward. And another.

He hurried to the end of the street, but he'd lost sight of Asia. She'd slipped away like a minnow after all.

She'd been heading toward the beach, of that he was sure.

Like that time I saw her crawling down the rocks, Will thought with a shiver. He remembered her, head down, legs and arms spread wide, spider-like. He knew that he'd have to follow her again. If he really was going crazy, he wanted to know. And if she was crazy, he wanted to know that, too.

He *had* to know. Will pulled out his cell phone. *Favor—find out info on Asia Marin,* he texted. Angus knew everyone and their dirt. If anyone could find out about Asia, it was someone at the *Gazette.*

It only took Angus a few moments to respond. *Poor kay?*

Will sighed. No wonder Angus had nearly flunked Spanish last year. *Need to know.*

;-) was Angus's response.

Okay, so he's not deep, Will thought. *Maybe that's a good thing. I've got enough depth to deal with right now.* He tucked his phone back into his pocket and hurried down the street. After a few steps, he moved into a dead trot.

The darkness was sudden as Will left the restaurants and shops behind him. It was as if he was entering a dark room. The sidewalk ended suddenly, as well, and he found himself following the edge of the road. Pebbles and rocks mixed with grass that had escaped from wide green lawns. He turned another corner, and there she was.

Asia walked on, the lights of the town fading behind her. Trees with dark limbs reached overhead like giants waiting to pluck them from the ground, eat them alive. Here the houses were closer to the road, but Asia passed them by. She walked another block, then two, then half a mile. Soon she headed down a curved street that Will knew led to the beach. Every now and again a lonely street lamp glowed solitary in the darkness.

Here, once again, houses stood behind tall hedges that grew improbably close to the sand and salt of the ocean. Asia paused at a driveway, peered beyond the leaf wall. Then she turned and stepped into the yard. Will followed to the edge of the drive but didn't dare go any farther, although there were no cars or people in evidence. The house was dark, and he could barely see her as she made her way up the front steps. She stopped at the door and turned—a ghostly shadow. He thought that he caught a glimpse of her green eyes before she placed her hand on the knob and stepped into the darkness.

Will stood watching for a long time. But no light in the house went on. Finally he turned. A small, tastefully carved placard at the end of the driveway proclaimed this to be the property of the Joyce family.

Will stared hard at the sign. *Isn't Asia's last name Marin?*

He had followed her hoping for clues, but all he got was more mystery.

Chapter Eight

From the Walfang Gazette
Police Blotter: Car Vandalized

3:24 am: Police were called to a residence at 94 White Oak Drive to investigate a car that was reportedly vandalized. The hood and sides of the white Lexus sustained scratches, broken windows, and slashed tires. No arrests have been made, although authorities claim to have several leads. . . .

Gretchen blew across the top of her coffee, inhaling the rich scent. She'd added some cinnamon, and it smelled like Christmas to her. Like the Christmases she used to have when her mom still lived with them. Gretchen didn't always drink coffee. Just on the mornings when she'd had trouble falling asleep the night before. Or when she'd been sleepwalking. She always woke up those mornings with a mind full of fuzz and a body that felt limp, like a flower that needed watering.

Her cat, Bananas, wandered into the kitchen. She rubbed against the table leg, then against Gretchen.

"You love me as much as you love the table?" Gretchen asked as she reached down to scratch behind Bananas' ears. "Hm? That much?"

Bananas's eyes were slitted. She sprang onto Gretchen's lap, purring, and lifted her face to Gretchen's nose.

"Oh, *more* than the table, now?"

A sharp knock at the door, and the cat scrambled off of Gretchen's lap, tearing at her with unguarded claws as she bolted to the floor and streaked out of the room.

"Ouch." Gretchen sucked in her breath as she inspected the long, raised scratch on the inside of her thigh.

"Sorry." Will's shape was hazy through the screen door. Gretchen waved at him to come in.

"She doesn't know her own strength."

"Does it hurt?" He reached toward Gretchen's thigh, but she dropped the hem of her short pajama bottoms and crossed her legs. Will flushed with sudden embarrassment. He looked down at his hands, as if he were grateful to have something in them. "I, uh, I brought your newspaper in." He dropped it on the table.

"What's up? What brings you by at this early hour?"

"You're always up early."

"That doesn't mean I'm expecting visitors. I'm still in my pajamas, aren't I?"

Will sighed. "You're hard to argue with."

"Tell it to my dad. So, what's up?"

Will shook his head. "I'm not sure." He narrowed his eyes at her. "Did you break up with Jason?"

Gretchen felt the back of her neck get hot. "What? Why?"

"Just . . . I heard something."

"You heard something? From who? Asia?"

Will lifted his eyebrows. "Have you been talking to Asia?"

"Of course. I mean, we work together. But she was there when Jason came in. And when he went out." Gretchen shrugged. "How do you know about that?"

"How much do you know about Asia?"

"Not much."

"Not much, like . . ."

Gretchen hesitated, her mind a twisted jungle of thoughts. Did she know anything about Asia? At work, it was usually Asia who asked most of the questions. She didn't really give up information about herself. Gretchen studied Will's face. "Why are you so interested in Asia?"

Will sighed, sat back in his chair. He looked at the clock on the wall. Ten seconds clicked by. "There's something . . . I don't know, strange about her."

Gretchen spoke carefully. "She's just shy."

"Shy? Not quite."

"She doesn't talk much."

"That's not the same thing as being shy."

"I guess I don't know what you're looking for." Gretchen heard the heat in her own voice. She took a sip of coffee to calm down. She wrapped her hands around the mug, surprised at the power of her own feelings. She didn't want to be having this conversation. She didn't want Will to be asking these questions about Asia. Besides, Gretchen had her own questions.

How had Asia stopped Jason in his tracks like that? As if her words—or was it her voice?—had a power of its own.

Gretchen looked down at the pile of mail on the table, pretending to be interested in it. She could feel Will's eyes studying her.

"Okay," he said at last.

Gretchen riffled through the mail. She spotted a postmark and pulled a letter out of the pile. She knew the handwriting.

"What is it?" Will asked.

"Nothing," Gretchen said. She met Will's eyes. "It's from my mother."

They both stared at the letter as if it were a poison thing.

"Are you going to open it?" Will asked.

Gretchen took a sip of her coffee, shook her head.

Will cocked his head. "Has she written to you before?"

Gretchen shrugged. "A couple of times a year."

"And you just—you don't read the letters?"

"Not yet."

"But you will?"

"God, Will, I'm not your science project, okay?" Gretchen snapped. "If my mother has anything to say, she can call. She can Skype. She can get on a plane and come talk to me. She has enough money." A dart of guilt stabbed at Gretchen—she hadn't meant to growl at Will. But she didn't really feel like discussing the situation with her mother. Yvonne had kept everything in the divorce. Gretchen didn't blame her. Not exactly. After all, her mother had a ton of family money.

But then she'd moved to France and just left them. And Gretchen's father hadn't wanted to accept the reality that without Yvonne's money, their lifestyle just wasn't sustainable. Johnny's income wasn't enough to cover private school, rent, and expenses in Manhattan. Yet for years Johnny had just kept digging the hole that started when Yvonne left. He'd dug until they didn't have a choice anymore. Johnny had inherited the house on Long Island from his father. He owned it free and clear, so they were going to live in it. "I'm sorry, Will, I just can't deal with all of that right now."

Will frowned at the bitterness in her voice. "Okay," he said. It was a retreat, and it sounded like one. "So," Will went on, switching gears, "are we going to that party tonight?"

"I thought you didn't want to go."

"I don't."

"But you're doing it to cheer me up?"

"Is it going to work?"

Gretchen gave him a lopsided smile. "Probably."

Will sighed. "That's what I was afraid of."

"So I'm picking you up at nine?"

"I said I'd go—not that I'd be willing to get stuck there all night. I'll meet you."

"You'd better show up."

"Have I ever let you down?"

Gretchen thought it over. "Yes."

"Not since eighth grade. And I would've called that time—I just didn't have a cell phone."

"If that's the story you're sticking with . . ."

Will stood up. "I'll be there," he promised.

Gretchen nodded. She picked up her mug of coffee and took a sip. It wasn't hot anymore, just a comfortable, warm temperature. "Good," she said. "Now get out of here. I have to go to work."

Will pointed to her leg. "Don't forget to put something on that scratch."

She'd forgotten all about the cat. At the mention of the scratch, it started to throb. "Love hurts," Gretchen said.

Will nodded. "Tell me about it."

Gretchen scanned the press of bodies, searching for Will. *Not here.* She sighed. *I never should have agreed to let him meet me,* she thought. Who knew when he would arrive? And she'd be stuck standing around by herself, or else mingling with people she didn't like. *Why did I want to come here?* she wondered. That was the problem with parties—they seemed to promise fun and diversion, but in reality they usually only offered boring conversations with the same people she'd been avoiding.

"Gretchen!" Harry Ansell waved and pushed his way through the partygoers to greet her. He was wearing a navy polo shirt, khaki shorts, and expensive-looking pair of leather sandals, and he looked like what he was—a nice but not too smart prep school kid on his way to a second-tier college in the fall. Gretchen had never known him well, but they had been friendly over the years. They showed up at a lot of the same parties in the city, traveled in the same circles.

"Hey, Ansell," Gretchen said. Hardly anyone ever called Harry by his first name.

Ansell surprised her with a friendly hug. "God, I'm glad you came." He looked her in the eye. "I just want you to know that Jason isn't coming."

The words were meant kindly, but to Gretchen, they held the sting of a slap that had caught her off guard. It had somehow never occurred to her that Jason might be here. Maybe because Ansell had existed in her Walfang universe so much longer than Jason had. Gretchen had known Ansell since they were small. He belonged to the Walfang that held Will and Tim and Angus. Jason was a rocky satellite that existed at the edge of her orbit—she thought of him as her own moon, not as a planet with orbits of his own.

"After I heard about what happened at Bella's, I called him and told him not to show his face here." Ansell shook his head. "He tried to play it off like he was some victim, but I was like, 'Hey, I know Gretchen, okay?' "

Gretchen nodded, her head swimming. "Thank you."

"Don't sweat it. Hey, Angus is around here somewhere. . . . Oh! Hey, here's Trina. You guys know each other, right?"

Trina detached herself from a pair of preppy worshippers and made her way over to join Gretchen. "Hello, Gretchen," Trina said. Her mouth smiled, but her eyes stayed cold.

"Hi." Gretchen squirmed uncomfortably, cursing herself for coming to this party without backup. She hadn't returned Trina's texts in days.

"Ansell!" someone shouted. Ansell gave Gretchen a friendly pat on the arm and plunged back into the crowd of partygoers.

"So, I guess you've been busy." Trina didn't smile.

"Yeah." Gretchen didn't feel like inventing excuses, but she was more than happy to take the one Trina offered.

"So . . . I talked to Jason."

"Oh?" Gretchen was surprised, even though she knew she shouldn't be. *He sure moved on fast.*

Trina's lips curled into a smug smile of ownership. "Someone trashed his car—did you hear that?"

"What?"

"Yeah—he's stuck driving his parents' car—the Lexus is slashed up. Jason thought you might know something about it."

Gretchen couldn't speak, couldn't move. She felt welded into place. *Jason suspects me?* The news had shocked her; the accusation shocked her more. "No," she finally managed to strangle out. "I didn't even—I had no idea."

"Really?" Trina sounded dubious. Her eyes flicked over Gretchen's shoulder.

Gretchen turned. Asia was standing several feet away, near a railing wrapped in cords of tiny white lights. She was watching them.

Trina gave Gretchen one last up-and-down glance and walked off to rejoin her group of admirers. She said something to the preppy boys, and one of them turned to look at Gretchen. She felt herself blush with embarrassment and anger.

Asia put a hand on Gretchen's shoulder. "Their thoughts can't touch you."

The words washed over Gretchen like a cool wave. She turned to face her friend. "You know, my mother used to always say, 'Sticks and stones may break my bones, but words can never hurt me.'" Gretchen sighed. "But that isn't true."

"They only hurt when you care," Asia said.

Gretchen walked over to where Asia had been standing. "I guess that's my problem." She leaned against the railing, looking down at the dark water. Clusters of silver stars—the reflection of the tiny white lights—shone up at her, shimmering in the liquid blackness. A breeze blew up against her, cooling the sweat on her arms. It was a sultry night, and the bodies pressed close together on the pier created enough heat to make Gretchen's red cotton sundress stick to her back. She lifted her thick hair off her neck, feeling a trickle creep down her spine. She turned toward Asia. "I wasn't expecting to see you here."

Asia looked down at the water. She seemed as if she was considering how to respond. "I'm keeping an eye on someone," she confessed.

Gretchen laughed. "Thanks."

Asia cocked her head, a quizzical smile playing at her lips. "You think it's you?"

"Isn't it?"

Asia shrugged. "Perhaps," she said. Her eyes sparkled, as if Gretchen amused her.

No wonder Will was asking about her. Gretchen was starting to have questions of her own. "You're so . . ." Gretchen searched for the right word. "Strange."

Asia laughed, and Gretchen blushed.

"I don't mean that you're strange," Gretchen said quickly. "I just mean you're—you know—kind of mysterious."

"I'm not offended," Asia said.

Silence settled between them. The party grew around them, the hot press of bodies encroaching on their space. "It's hot here," Asia said after a few moments. "How can you breathe?"

An arm brushed against Gretchen as a short, squat guy pressed past, fighting his way toward the beer. "It's better here at the edge."

"There's no room."

Gretchen shoved out an elbow, and someone retreated. A few inches appeared, and Asia slipped into the space. "It makes you want to dive in," she said, looking down at the water.

"In that dress?" Gretchen joked.

Asia looked down at her white dress. It was goddess-style—halter at the top, gathers of white fabric down almost to her ankles.

"Not the best for a swim," Gretchen pointed out.

"Hm." Asia looked down at the water again, seeming to barely hear her. She narrowed her eyes suddenly, as if she saw something, and pulled back.

"What is it?"

Asia looked at her with cool green eyes. "Do you see anything?"

Gretchen studied the water. "No."

"No," Asia repeated.

Gretchen studied her friend's face but couldn't read anything there. Over Asia's shoulder, Gretchen noticed a handsome dark-skinned guy checking Asia out. Her exotic looks had been attracting quite a bit of attention, and Gretchen had to check a pang of jealousy. *The* other *reason Will was asking about her.*

"I have to step away from here," Asia said suddenly. "This heat . . ."

"Really?" Even in the press of people, Asia seemed cool and unmussed.

But Asia was already moving away, gliding past bodies and moving steadily toward the end of the pier. Gretchen watched her move. It was as if there were a force field around her. She collided with no one, and no one touched her.

"Someone's looking at you." Angus appeared at Gretchen's side, holding a plastic cup half full of foam. He slipped into the space that Asia had left.

"Who?"

Angus nodded, and Gretchen spotted a pale boy in a black T-shirt and jeans. His huge eyes met hers for a moment, then flicked away.

"Oh, that guy," Gretchen said vaguely. "Kirk the crazy screaming sophomore." She watched as he picked up an empty beer cup and tossed it into the water. Then another. He reached for a third, but a girl snatched it away. She wasn't finished with it, apparently. Kirk cringed and skulked away, octopus-like, reaching out his arms and legs along the railing and feeling his way backward.

"Crazy is right."

"Local celebrity."

"Hey, he gets his picture in the paper more than Lindsay Lohan."

Gretchen laughed. A stray lock of hair blew across her face, and Angus reached for it, then drew his hand away, tentatively. "Sorry," he mumbled. He leaned against the railing, his body weight on his arms, and stared down at the water.

Gretchen smoothed the hair out of her face and looked up at him, smiling ruefully. *I guess I can't expect things to go right back to normal with Angus.*

"Where's Jason?" Angus asked, giving her a sideways look.

Gretchen put her hands over her face and groaned. "Don't mention that name."

"Yeah, that's what I heard." He smiled down at the water.

"Word gets around."

Angus shrugged and turned to face her. "Jason has friends. I heard your waitress friend stood up for you."

"I guess."

"What's her name—Asia, right?"

"Right."

"Is she here tonight?"

"Somewhere." Gretchen scanned the crowd, but

the white dress had disappeared. "Why—you interested?" She blushed a little the minute the words were out of her mouth, but decided not to dig the hole deeper.

Angus scoffed. "Get serious."

"She's so gorgeous, though."

"More like scary."

"Really?" Gretchen blinked up at him. She thought about Asia's green eyes, her long black hair. She *was* a little cold; then again, that was part of what Gretchen liked about her. She got the feeling that with Asia there weren't any lies.

Angus watched her face for a moment. He seemed as if he was about to say something, then seemed to change his mind. "Is Will coming?"

"Allegedly."

"No evidence?"

"Not so far." Gretchen looked out at the shore. Beyond the dunes, the mansion was lit up, spewing light almost to the sand. The lights from the pier glowed to the water, leaving the waterline in gray shadow. The sand was dotted with dark shapes—couples who had escaped the hot, sweaty party to make some heat of their own.

"So you're stuck with me?" Angus asked.

"I guess it's you or Kirk." Gretchen looked over toward the skinny boy. He was having an animated conversation with someone—someone invisible. The passion in his face gave Gretchen the creeps.

"Someone needs to do an intervention with that kid."

"Then what would everyone talk about?" Gretchen asked. "The paper wouldn't have anything to publish."

Angus nodded. "Yeah. Still, I feel sorry for him."

"Why don't his parents do something?"

"His mother's always down at the bar with her shady boyfriend, the dealer. His father's dead. His sister's the only sane one. But Adelaide's only twenty. What's she gonna do?"

They stood there, side by side, looking down at the water. Below them, a ghostly figure moved away from the pier, along the stretch of wet sand. The water raced to meet her bare feet, spilling up around her ankles. Gretchen could tell by her movements as well as her long dark hair that it was Asia. Her white dress seemed to shimmer, like the lights in the water below, as she faded slowly into the darkness. Gretchen sighed, wondering when everything had gotten so complicated.

Will watched her watching the water for a few moments. A wave reached out, embracing her feet with gently hissing bubbles. She sank slightly in the sand before the water sucked back toward the sea. The hem of her white dress was wet, but she didn't seem to care. She was looking out over the dark horizon.

Will was behind her, sitting on the sand in the semidarkness. He had been sitting there for at least half an hour. He'd promised Gretchen that he would go to the party, but the nearer he got, the heavier his footsteps became. Will hated yelling small talk over loud music.

He hated being shoved up against people he didn't know. Tim had always been the fun brother—the one who loved people.

Will's head was full of Tim tonight. Here, at the edge of the water, the memories of their last night together came fast and thick. . . .

"Will, where's your brother?" his father had asked as he banged in through the back door. "I told him I needed his help with the tractor."

Will shoved his chair away from the table. "I can do it."

"Bert, for heaven's sake, don't bother with that now." Will's mother shot her husband a look from the sink, where she was trimming sugar snap peas. "Will, I need you to finish chopping those tomatoes. And Bert, go wash up—you're covered in grease. We're ready to eat in ten minutes."

"Woman, you boss me around like you're the queen of England," Will's father said playfully.

She flicked a kitchen towel at him. "I'm the queen of the house."

"Yes, Your Highness."

"It's Your *Majesty*," she corrected.

"Got it." Will's dad winked at him and headed down the hall to wash up.

Will took the tomatoes to the stove and added them to the pan, where onions were already browning. The pulpy juice immediately began to bubble and turn orange around the edges in the sweet butter.

"Thanks, Will. Would you go find Tim for me? Let him know that we're about to eat?"

"Sure." Will loped upstairs, then climbed the ladder and poked his head up through the floor. "Tim?"

No answer.

Will climbed up to the top. Tim had converted the attic to his room the year before. It had low ceilings and only two tiny windows. But from the windows, there was a beautiful sweeping view. To the left were dunes and beyond that the sea. To the right was the bay. Tim spent hours up there, reading or playing the guitar. It was a cozy space, and Will often joined his brother there for long talks.

Will walked over to the window and looked down over the farmland below. The rows of iris had just begun to explode into ribbons of vibrant colors. Flowers were a lucrative crop, and these sat next to the thick, bushy heirloom tomatoes—just flowers, no fruit yet—and the smaller rows of sage, thyme, and dill. To the left was the bluff, and beyond the rows were the dunes, and then the sea. Will saw two figures down there. One was Tim. The other, with long blond hair lit by the setting sun, was Gretchen.

Will hesitated a moment, watching them. They seemed deep in conversation. He wondered what they were saying. Will knew how Tim felt about Gretchen—everyone knew. And Will could only assume that Gretchen felt the same way. Of course she loved Tim. Will had always feared that he would end up the third wheel instead of the third Musketeer. Maybe this year would be the year. . . .

"Will!" Mrs. Archer called up the stairs. "Tell Tim he has two minutes!"

Will hustled down the stairs and out the door. He cut across the fields between two rows of beans dotted with small white flowers along the vines. But by the time he'd reached the sand, Tim was alone.

He'd been standing at the edge of the water, watching the waves. Just as Asia watched them now.

Will stood looking at her, wondering what to say.

"I know you're there," she whispered after a moment, although she didn't turn to look at him.

"All right," he said, and she whipped around to face him. Her sandals fell into the retreating water with a splash.

Will hurried to retrieve them, and Asia's face had somewhat recovered by the time he handed them—crusted with sand—back to her.

"Thank you." She spoke to the sandals rather than to him.

He looked at her carefully. "You seem surprised to see me."

Asia looked up at him, but didn't speak. Will felt a tremble of doubt. He'd been sure that she'd been talking to him, but now he wondered if the words "I know you're there" could have been meant for someone else.

"You didn't like the party?" He stood close to her, so close that the top of her head was level with his chin. His body burned with the desire to brush that hair with his lips.

"It was too hot." She looked up at him. "Too many bodies."

He felt her voice, like music, through his body. He looked down into her eyes. "Can you explain to me how someone as small as you could intimidate someone as large as Jason Detenber?"

She went rigid. "What?"

The word was a clang—like a door slamming. It shook him, and Will blinked. "Gretchen told me what happened."

"Did she?" Her voice had gone soft again, musical.

Will felt sleepy, but he fought it. "She did."

"Are you certain?" It was a long note, almost a song.

Just agree, whispered a voice in his mind. But he couldn't let it go. There were too many holes in his memory—too many questions. He needed some answers. "Yes."

Asia cocked her head. She looked at him a long time. He had almost given up when she said, "You're different."

"What?" Will was so surprised by this that he took a step backward. "What do you mean?"

"There aren't many like you, Will."

Will didn't know what to say. "I'm nothing special."

Asia just looked at him. "Most . . . people . . . have weak minds."

"You say 'people' as if you aren't one of us."

"Life is full of mysteries," Asia said at last. She held his gaze, but just for a moment, and then she kissed him on the jaw.

Before he even realized what happened, she was walking away across the sand. Will put a hand to his forehead. His brain was muddy, as if he'd just walked across a clear river, stirring up silt. He watched the white form as it began to fade from view. “You don't have to be so mysterious all the time!” he shouted after her.

But she didn't turn back.

Will sighed. He looked over at the pier. Gretchen and Angus were leaning against the railing, talking and smiling. *Would she even really notice if I skipped the party?* But Will knew that she would. He didn't want to go, but it wasn't worth hurting her feelings.

The sand rasped softly underfoot as he headed toward his friends. As he approached the pier, the gentle roar of the sea beside him subsided, giving way to sounds of music and laughter.

“Will!” Gretchen, half dangling over the side of the railing, waved frantically at him. He waved back, and hurried his steps toward the pier.

She fought her way through a thicket of moist bodies to reach him at the end of the pier, near the sand. “You made it,” she said. Her cheeks were pink from the heat, and her smile lit up her whole face. Her hair was loose around her shoulders, and she was wearing a pretty red halter dress. He was taken off guard at how beautiful she was. Usually Gretchen was just . . . Gretchen. But here, with her hair blowing in the soft breeze, she looked different to him.

Angus had gotten caught by Gina Abernathy—the chattiest girl in Walfang—and it took him a moment to extricate himself. “Hey, man,” he said, appearing at Gretchen's side. “A couple of people are talking about building a bonfire on the beach. What do you think?”

Someone screamed from the other end of the pier,

and that was when Will saw the figure standing atop the railing at the edge. Someone reached out as the figure spread its arms wide.

"Holy—"

Splash.

"Gretchen!" She was already running toward the end of the pier, and Will darted after her. "Gretchen!" She stopped at the railing and looked out over the edge.

The figure in the water splashed and writhed.

"Shit." Will kicked off his shoes. There were screams and movement around him. A hand grabbed at his shirt as Will climbed over the rail, but he pushed it away.

"Stop him!" Gretchen's voice.

"Will!" Angus's voice came to him from far away.

Below, Will saw white foam around the frantic figure. Someone threw a life preserver into the water, but the figure ignored it.

"It's Kirk Worstler," Angus said, and then Will stepped into the open air. For a moment he was weightless as he plunged, feet first, into the water.

Will heard someone—Gretchen?—screaming his name, but in a few quick strokes he had reached the life preserver. Grabbing it, he kicked until he was face to face with Kirk. Kirk's eyes were black, pupils dilated wide, and his dark hair streamed down his face.

"They're coming. They're almost here," Kirk spluttered as a slight wave caught him in the mouth. "They've come for her."

"What?" Will reached out, but Kirk slapped his hand away.

"Vengeance rushes from the mouths of the serpents. They've come for her—will she breathe fire on them?" Kirk looked at him. "They've tasted your blood."

"Who?"

"The seekriegers are singing. They've come for her. Can you hear them? Can you hear them?"

"No, dude. No—I can't hear them."

"No?" Only Kirk's head was visible above the water, eyes huge, pale skin. "You don't hear them?" He looked vulnerable, like a child.

"Will," said a voice.

It was Asia. Her head floated on the water nearby, hair slicked away from her face.

Kirk started screaming, and Will had to pin his arms to his sides. Reaching out, Asia touched Kirk's hair. He struggled away from her, but she leaned forward and sang something into his ear. Will couldn't catch the words—they were on his deaf side.

After a moment Kirk quieted. Then he seemed to lapse into a state of semiconsciousness.

"It's time to go back," Will told him. He gestured toward the shore.

Kirk had grown very still. Only his legs still beat the water, keeping him afloat. Will took loosened his grip and gently led Kirk to the red and white life preserver.

"I'm behind you," Asia said.

"Won't they be angry?" Kirk asked dreamily as Will kicked his way toward the shore.

"Who?"

"The seekriegers."

Will didn't know what that meant. "I don't think so," seemed like the safest answer.

"Good." Kirk seemed to sink a little, and his eyelids drooped. "I'm so tired."

"We're close now."

"I can't hear them anymore."

"That's okay."

A few of the partygoers watched from the pier, but most had gathered by the shore as Will and Kirk staggered out of the surf. Once he was back on his legs, Kirk's body started to sag a little, and Will had to hold him up.

Will helped Kirk to the sand, where he sat shivering, knees to chin. "The seekriegers have come for her. The song sleeps on the wind, waiting for deliverance. . . ."

Gina appeared with a towel, which she wrapped around Kirk's shoulders as he babbled on. People gathered around in a big circle, whispering and talking.

"Would you give him some room?" Will snapped.

Nobody did.

Will turned, expecting to see Asia nearby, but she was nowhere to be found. *Was she even really there?* he wondered. *Or did I dream that?* With his eyes, Will measured the distance from the shore to the place where Kirk had jumped. It was significant. *Asia must be a strong swimmer.*

"Will, hey—" It was Harry Ansell. His eyes were worried beneath his thick, straight brows. "Listen, would you . . . would you mind taking Kirk home?" He swept his five-hundred-dollar shaggy haircut out of his eyes. "Before the cops get here, I mean?"

"Will!" Gretchen was sprinting toward him. Angus loped behind her.

"Will—what the hell?" She punched him in the arm, hard. "What do you think you're doing? That drug addict could've killed you!"

"You don't even know the kid." Will thought about the gentleness in Kirk's face, the fear. "He might be crazy, but I don't think he's on anything."

"I can't believe this," Gretchen snapped. She stalked off across the sand, toward the parking lot. Will wanted to run after her, but he was too tired. He knew she was just worried about him and that she'd calm down. Eventually.

Will looked at his friends. Ansell seemed worried. And Angus was watching Kirk, who had curled up into a ball and fallen asleep beneath the towel.

"Why did he jump?" Ansell asked.

"I don't know—some crazy shit. Something about sea critters."

Angus looked at him sharply. "Seekriegers?"

"What? Yeah. Why—is that a thing?"

Angus shrugged. "I don't know. My grandfather used to talk about them."

"What are they?"

"Mermaids or something. He used to tell me all of these stories. . . ."

"Like what?"

Angus shook his head. "Sorry, dude, it was a long time ago. But maybe my grandmother remembers."

"Could we go talk to her tomorrow?"

Will knew that he must have sounded pretty desperate, because Angus was giving him a concerned look. "Sure, man. Whatever you want."

"Maybe in the morning, before I have to work."

"What am I going to do with this?" Ansell asked, watching Kirk sleep peacefully on the sand.

"Call his sister," Angus suggested. "She's used to cleaning up Kirk's messes."

"If I see a single word of this in the paper tomorrow . . . ," Ansell warned.

"You'll what?" Angus smirked. "Buy a copy for your parents?"

"Please don't do this to me."

Angus looked offended. "Dude—what kind of a guy do you think I am?"

"Thanks, man." Ansell walked back toward the pier.

"Seriously, you're not running the story?" Will asked as he and Angus headed toward the parking lot. Will was not looking forward to riding home all wet on his motorcycle.

"Of *course* I'm doing a story," Angus replied. He grinned. "Dude—what kind of a guy do you think I am? By the way, I looked into that thing."

"What thing? You mean Asia?"

"Yeah—I dug around a little."

"What did you find out?"

"I found out that she's a total black hole." Angus carefully unlocked the door of his rusted old Ford. This was the kind of thing that always used to crack Tim up—Angus locking his crappy old car when it was surrounded by Audis, Jaguars, Lexuses, Porsches. "The only thing I found out about Asia Marin is that she worked at Bella's last summer and came back this year. No known address. No phone number. No school records, dude."

"What about the Joyce family?" Will had e-mailed Angus the information he'd gotten from following Asia.

"They're from the city. Fischer and Julia. They have two kids, both in their thirties. Neither one named Asia."

"So—what does that mean?"

Angus shrugged. "It means that she's house-sitting. It means she's from somewhere else and comes here for the summer. No big mystery, I guess."

"Yeah," Will agreed. "No big mystery." But he couldn't keep the irony out of his voice.

Angus folded himself into his tiny car and waved before driving off. Will had just started toward his motorcycle when a movement caught his eye. It was a figure in white—Asia. She was at the far end of the driveway, walking away from the party at a rapid clip. Her dress was still damp and clung to her body, although it was dry enough so that the skirt fluttered at her ankles.

Will took off after her at a dead trot. His wet jeans made a *swish-swish* as he hurried after her.

The ground rose slightly as they headed away from the Ansell house. He was breathing heavily as he followed her, but she moved along, seemingly untroubled. Will heard a rumble behind him. He stepped aside to let the car pass. Asia didn't bother.

She didn't look back or slow her gait as the car swerved around her.

He heard another rumble, and a car zoomed past him. It was a blue BMW. It raced forward and pulled to a stop at the top of the bridge. Jason stepped out and walked toward the railing, blocking Asia's path.

For a moment, Will was frozen in place. He saw Jason's hulking form step forward. He heard him say something to Asia, but Will couldn't hear what it was. Asia opened her mouth to reply. "Shut up!" he snarled as he backed her toward the railing. "If it wasn't you, then tell me who it was!"

"Hey!" Will shouted. He started forward at a dead run.

Jason looked over toward the shout, his face registering surprise. Just then Asia twisted backward, snakelike, over the railing, kicked Jason in the chest, and went over the side.

Jason stood there, his arms full of empty air. He raced to the rail, but Asia had already disappeared into the water.

Jason turned to Will, horror written across his face.

"Jason!" Will shouted, "Stop!" But Jason was already getting back into his car. His tires smoked as he peeled away from the bridge.

Will reached the top of the bridge. He stared down at the water. It was a long, long fall. It was the kind of fall that killed people.

But Jason hadn't seen what Will had seen. Asia had flipped over the railing. Then she'd straightened out, her arms stretched over her head. She'd entered the water like an arrow, with hardly a splash. The slight wave folded over her feet like an envelope.

Will looked out over the water. Far down the river, close to where it entered the bay, he thought he saw a head rise out of the water. Hair fanned around it for a moment as the face glanced back at the bridge.

Then it sank into the river and disappeared.

Chapter Nine

From the Walfang Gazette
Theft at Miller Gallery

An eighteenth-century painting disappeared from the Miller Gallery last Tuesday. "I just walked in and noticed a blank spot on the wall," said gallery director Don Beltran yesterday. The painting had been on loan as part of the "Gifts of the Sea" exhibit, on display until September 15. . . .

Gretchen watched the creamer tumble to the bottom of the iced coffee, leaving a trail of ghostly white in its wake. She stirred the liquid with a straw and took a sip, hoping it would wake her up, if not lift her mood.

"Hon, you're concentrating a little bit too hard on that coffee and not enough on table fourteen," Lisette said as she swept past, a heavy tray in her hand.

Gretchen looked up, registering the father and two young sons who had descended into her section. She took a swig of her drink, then tucked it behind the counter and went out to greet her customers. They wanted Belgian waffles with strawberries on top, and she took the orders automatically and stuck them onto the board for Angel.

"Wake up, Gretchen," he snapped at her. "You look like a zombie."

"Thanks," Gretchen replied. Her body felt too heavy, her mind too numb, to think of a witty reply.

"Oh, lay off, Angel," Lisette called from across the diner.

Gretchen grabbed her coffee and took another swig. Asia was sorting silverware nearby, smiling as Angel muttered to himself. "How does she get away with it?" Gretchen asked, half to herself.

"Lisette?" Asia looked up. "You mean, why doesn't Angel get angry with her teasing?"

"Yeah. If anyone else talked that way to him, he'd be pissed."

Asia shrugged. "He's in love with her."

"*What?* Oh my God, I thought they hated each other!"

Asia laughed softly. "No. They're getting married next summer."

"Whoa—I had *no* idea." Gretchen sneaked a glance at sour-looking Angel, a prisoner behind his window. He was scowling at the waffle iron. "How did you find that out?"

"Sometimes people just tell me things."

"I'm going on break, ladies." Lisette pulled off her apron and stuffed it into a cubby behind the counter. "Anyone want anything from Conrad's?"

"Get me a pack of that gum you're always smacking." This was from Angel.

"Was I asking you? See you all in fifteen." Lisette gave them a toodle-loo wave and headed toward the rear.

Gretchen noticed the smile Lisette and Angel

exchanged just before she pushed open the back door. She wondered how many of those glances she had missed.

Taking another pull of coffee, Gretchen reached for her notebook. A paper fell out, fluttering to the floor. Asia reached down to get it. "Good news?" she asked as she handed it back to Gretchen, face down.

Gretchen let one shoulder rise, then dip. "It's just—a letter from my mother."

The clean spoons clinked as Asia dropped them into their compartment. She didn't speak or even look at Gretchen.

"She wants me to come live with her . . . in Paris."

Asia nodded as she reached for the knives. "Will you go?"

"I don't . . . I don't know." Gretchen tucked the paper into the notebook.

Asia nodded. "It's not really about choosing one place or another, is it?" Her eyes held Gretchen's.

"I've never been close to my mother," Gretchen admitted. "She's . . ." Gretchen shook her head, unsure how to describe Yvonne. "She isn't my birth mother."

"Does that matter?" Asia asked.

"Not really. My dad isn't my birth dad, either, and I'm close to him. But I just think that she never really saw me as her daughter. She just saw me as this . . . person."

Asia considered this. "But living with her might give you an opportunity to get to know her."

"Or it might make me insane," Gretchen countered. "And it would probably break my dad's heart."

"It sounds like you don't want to go," Asia said.

"Not particularly."

"And yet you're carrying around this letter."

Gretchen sighed. "I guess I'm not sure I want to stay here, either." She felt the pressure building in her throat.

Asia placed a hand on Gretchen's arm. "The memories will follow you," she said. Her voice was soft and somehow comforting, although the words were disturbing. *The memories will follow me,* Gretchen thought, and in an instant she was back on the beach. Her vision was filled with fire.

It was night, and the sail of Tim's boat was in flames. Will was lying on the sand beside her, unconscious, and Gretchen was shivering in wet clothes. She didn't know how she'd gotten there. She didn't know how the fire had started. All she knew was that she was terrified. Gretchen checked to make sure that Will was alive. But when she heard the police sirens, she left Will on the shore and ran through the darkness to her own home. She heard Guernsey barking in the background as she sneaked quietly into her room. She peeled off her wet clothes and tossed them into the washing machine before her father realized anything was wrong.

Gretchen had desperately wanted to tell Will everything, but she didn't know how. Part of her was terrified that Will would blame her for Tim's death. *And maybe I am guilty,* Gretchen thought. That was the most frightening part—she didn't know for sure.

"Gretchen!" Angel yelled. Gretchen jumped, startled. She turned and saw him glowering. "Order up."

With a shaking hand, Gretchen grabbed the three Belgian waffles and delivered them to table fourteen.

When she got back to the counter, she saw that Asia had refilled her iced coffee. "Thanks," Gretchen said.

"I'm back!" Lisette called as she bustled through the rear door. "Got your gum, you jerk." She tucked it into the rear pocket of Angel's hideous black-and-white-checked pants. She stuffed her purse into the cubby and pulled out her apron. "What did I miss?" she asked as she tied the apron strings.

Me spilling my guts out to Asia, Gretchen thought.

"We were just talking," Asia said at last.

"Well, chat time's over, toots," Lisette told her. "Those ladies just sat in your section."

"Back to work," Asia said as she got to her feet. She gave Gretchen a warm glance and a gentle pat on the shoulder.

Gretchen watched as Asia glided over to the older women. They smiled up at her as if she were a friend. *Sometimes people just tell me things,* Asia had said.

People, Gretchen thought. *Like me.*

"Gran!" Angus called as they slammed in through the back door and straight into the kitchen. "Gran!"

A white cockatiel in a cage squawked at them from its perch near the refrigerator. The house smelled stale, but the kitchen was tidy. Angus's grandmother didn't cook much.

"For God's sake, quit yelling." Angus's grandmother shuffled in from the living room, a cigarette in one hand and an ashtray in the other. "And stop calling me Gran. My name's Roberta." She perched primly onto a cushioned metal folding chair and gave Will the eye. "Who's this?"

"It's Will, Gran. You've met him a hundred times." Angus had his arm buried up to the elbow in a cookie jar shaped like a giant strawberry.

"Hello, Mrs. McFarlan."

Angus's grandmother took a long drag on her cigarette. Then she touched her bleached hair gingerly with a long, manicured nail. "You're the Archer boy," she said, eyeing his scar.

"Gran, you call these cookies?" Angus complained through a mouthful of Oreo crumbs. "They're stale!"

"Don't eat those; they're ancient. They'll probably kill you."

Angus swallowed. He'd already polished off three. "Eh, they're not awful. You want one?" This was directed at Will.

"I'm good."

"So, what brings you by?" Mrs. McFarlan peered at her grandson with a keen eye as the cockatiel pecked at itself in a mirror. "Don't tell me you came for the Oreos."

"I was wondering if you remembered any of those old stories that Gramps used to tell—the ones about the seekriegers."

"Oh, those old stories." Mrs. McFarlan ground her cigarette into the ashtray, where the embers spread and scattered like dying stars. "I swear, Walfang fishermen are the most superstitious men in the entire world."

Angus lifted his eyebrows at Will. *You see?*

"So what were they?" Will asked. "Angus said mermaids?"

Mrs. McFarlan studied him for a moment, tapping her nails against the wooden tabletop. "Something like that. But not like mermaids in pictures. No fins or any of that crap. More like wild women of the sea."

"So you remember the stories," Angus prompted.

"I remember. Arthur always half believed in them, I think." The cockatiel had started making a racket, and Mrs. McFarlan crossed to the cage. "Come, sweetie, come out." She pursed her lips into a wet kiss and offered her finger to the cockatiel.

"So can you tell us about the seekriegers?" Angus pressed.

Mrs. McFarlan cried out, tearing her hand from the cage. A delicate drop of blood traced down her finger where the cockatiel had bitten her. Angus grabbed a flowered kitchen towel and held it out to his grandmother, but she just scowled at him and reached for a paper towel. "Lunatic bird," she grumbled as she pressed the towel against her finger.

"Sorry, Gran," Angus said.

"It's my right hand, too." Mrs. McFarlan shook her head as the cockatiel squawked and bobbed its head. "Everybody in this family's crazy." She narrowed her eyes up at Angus. "What do you want to know about the seekriegers for?"

"Just . . . I was trying to remember the stories." Angus's voice sounded feeble.

"It's because of me," Will interjected. "This guy I know thinks he saw one."

"This guy you know?"

"He may just be on drugs," Will admitted. "Or nuts."

"He *saw* one?" Mrs. McFarlan looked doubtful.

"He heard one," Will corrected.

The plastic cushion sighed as Mrs. McFarlan sat down heavily. "He heard one," she repeated. She thought a moment. Then she got up and left the room.

Will heard her footsteps retreat through the living room. Then boards creaked as she ascended the stairs.

Will and Angus looked at each other. The bird let out a squawk, then fell silent.

"Does your grandmother often just walk out of the room like that?" Will asked.

"Not usually."

"Should we leave?"

"I'm not sure," Angus admitted. But instead of heading for the door, he crossed to the refrigerator. "Oh, great, lemonade." He pulled out the carton and checked it. "It hasn't even expired yet." He poured some into a glass, chugged it, and poured himself another glass. Then he got down another for Will and filled it half full. "It's finished, dude—sorry."

Will pulled out a chair and sat down on the maroon cushion. It was surprisingly comfortable for a folding chair. The table had a cushioned vinyl-covered top, too. Angus sat down in his grandmother's chair and set the mismatched glasses on the table. Will took a sip of the lemonade. It was cloyingly sweet, coating his tongue with sugar. But the cold felt good.

The boards creaked again, and then Mrs. McFarlan appeared in the doorway. She was tall and thin, like a blade of grass. She wore shorts that revealed skin sagging at the knee and an old pink T-shirt. With her short blond hair that was dark at the roots, she gave the impression of a flower that had stayed too long in a vase and started to fade in the sun. In her hand was a book.

"What's that, Gran?" Angus asked.

"This was written by your grandfather's grandfather." Mrs. McFarlan placed it gently on the table. "It probably belongs in some historical society, but Arthur never wanted to give it away."

Will reached out and touched the cover with a fingertip. It was hand-pressed leather, worn to a fossil by time. He looked at Mrs. McFarlan, and she nodded her approval. Slowly, slowly, he opened the cover. Turned to a page in the middle. The next had a heading: *July 15, 1884*. The page was crammed with tight, even writing.

"It's a captain's log," Mrs. McFarlan explained. "Arthur's grandfather was lost at sea at a young age. They found his boat broken apart on a sandbar not six miles from home."

"He was the captain?" Angus asked.

His grandmother nodded. "Rowan McFarlan, yes."

"Have you read it?" Angus asked her.

"I read it," she told him. "All it proves is that everyone in this family is nuts." But her voice was hollow.

Will could hardly bear to take his hand from the book. "May I take it?" he asked.

"I think you'd better." Mrs. McFarlan looked out the window. The light had dimmed in the room, and Will saw that dark clouds were gathering at the edge of the horizon. "At least we'll get a break from this heat," she said.

"We'd better get going before we get drenched," Angus said. He leaned over and gave his grandmother a kiss on the cheek. "Thanks, Gran."

She turned her sharp crow's gaze on Will. "I want that book back."

Will nodded. "Absolutely."

Angus held open the screen door. Will took a step toward it, but Mrs. McFarlan called him back.

"Keep an eye on that friend of yours," she told him. "The one who heard the seekriegers."

"I thought you said they didn't exist," Angus said.

She kept her eyes locked on Will. "Keep an eye on him," she repeated.

"I will." It felt like a promise between them.

Will and Angus stepped outside into the heavy air. Just as they settled into Angus's battered Ford, the rain started to pour from the sky. It skimmed over the windshield in a heavy sheet. Angus looked down at the book tucked safely on Will's lap. "This must be our lucky day," he said.

"Yeah," Will agreed, although he wasn't really sure he believed it.

Will didn't read the book for the next three days. It simply sat, indifferent, on the top of his bureau. Will was burning to read it. But he didn't want to read snatches here and there. He wanted to be alone with it, to study it.

But he didn't have the time. There were sunflowers to collect. The flowers were as tall as he was, and their cordlike stems were coated in prickly fuzz that left his hands raw. He collected tomatoes in the early morning, before the sun became desperate and fierce. He picked the crisp green lettuce and the arugula that could command top dollar with the foodies, then rinsed it in the enormous stainless-steel sink. Will pulled weeds, mulched with hay, made sure the chickens were fed. One morning Will noticed that the smallest one—the one with a twisted leg—had been pecked twice. Will dressed the two small raw wounds and separated her from the rest of the flock. He built a small cage for her with wood and chicken wire, and placed a roost in the corner. He felt sorry for her, alone in her cage, watching the other chickens with the longing of a lonely child kept inside while the others played. But what could he do? If he let her out among the flock, they would peck her to death.

And he worked at the stand. It was high season, and everything was selling. His mother's freshly baked scones and muffins were usually gone by nine-thirty in the morning. The stack of *New York Times* newspapers disappeared even earlier. The tomatoes, dahlias, blackberries, zucchini, peppers, yellow squash, corn . . . Will often stood for five hours straight behind the counter. He didn't have time to pee, so he tried not to drink anything early in the morning. Tim had once joked that he had to wear Depends on the days he was working the stand. Will was beginning to think that was a good idea.

The fourth morning, Will came downstairs early. His father was already at the breakfast table. His uncle Carl was there, too. The coffeepot gurgled and sputtered on the counter beside a mug his mother had set out for Will. A flowered china plate sat patiently on the table, a scone set neatly at the center. His mother had placed jars of homemade pear and strawberry jam on the table, along with real butter.

"Hey, Will!" Carl called, grinning hugely. "Good to see you, bedhead!"

His father sat at the other side of the square white table, eyeing him silently. He looked down at his plate, took another forkful of scrambled egg, and dipped it in a mound of ketchup. "You're lookin' tired," Will's father said.

"Slept badly," Will said as he poured the dark, fragrant coffee into the mug.

"Didn't sleep at all, more like," his father said.

"Teenagers are always up late," Carl said with a grin.

"Yeah." Will sank into the chair across from his father's and tore open his scone.

"Somethin' botherin' you?" Will's father asked. He looked up at Will with a strange mixture of curiosity and trepidation—as if he wanted to hear what was on Will's mind but was afraid of what it might be.

Will had a sudden desire to tell his father everything. He couldn't explain it, but he really felt like his father was *listening.* "Dad, have you ever heard of . . . sea witches?"

"Witches?"

"Or . . . seekriegers?"

"What?" Will's father exchanged a wary glance with Carl. Will's uncle got busy eating a piece of sausage.

"Never mind." Will spread strawberry jam on the scone very precisely. He couldn't meet his father's gaze. He sounded crazy. He knew it.

"What are you asking?" Will's father was holding a fork in one hand, a knife in the other, and watching Will intensely.

"It's just—I've heard some stories lately." Will shrugged and gave a half laugh, trying to make it seem as if the whole thing were a joke. "Crazy stories, I guess."

His father set his fork and knife down carefully. He took a long pull of his coffee and sat silent as a stone.

Will picked at his scone. It was still warm from the oven—moist and sweet, dotted with black currants. His mother made them every morning, along with muffins and cookies to sell at the stand. She got up at three to bake, then went back to bed at eight for a few hours.

Will usually liked the quiet mornings with his father, and he was always happy to see his uncle. Will's dad didn't believe in breakfast cereal—he said it was a conspiracy concocted by large corporations to make people eat garbage in the morning. He always made himself eggs and toast, and occasionally he would fry up some bacon. They would eat in companionable silence, then clean up and get to work.

But this morning the silence made Will squirm. His eye fell on the local newspaper, and he was reaching for it when his father said, "There's a lot of strange stories in this town."

"What?" Will was shocked.

"I've heard of the seekriegers," his father said quietly. He looked Will dead in the eye.

"And?" Will turned to his uncle. Carl looked as if he had something to say, but a glance from Will's father silenced him.

Will's father took his plate to the sink. His back was turned to Will when he said, "There's nothing to those tales, Will. Just a bunch of junk for simple minds." He dried his hands carefully and hung the flowered towel on a hook on the wall. "Come on, Carl," he said. Then he walked out the back door without another word.

Carl downed another plug of coffee. He gave Will an apologetic smile, then shoved in his chair and hurried after his brother.

That night Will took a shower and crawled into

bed. He turned out the light and tucked his feet under Guernsey's warm body. But he couldn't fall asleep. The moon shone like a searchlight into his room. It illuminated the bureau, and on top of that, the book, which crouched like an animal on the corner.

Guernsey didn't move as Will pushed back the covers and crossed the room. The book was heavy in his hands. He climbed back into bed, clicked on the small lamp on the table at his bedside, and turned to the first brittle page.

July 12, 1884

39° 21´ N, 52° 53´ W

I expect we are three weeks from port, fair skies, but the winds do not blow. The ELIZA THOMAS *is a fair craft, albeit small, and has the reputation of being a lucky ship, and I've enjoyed captaining her.*

I haven't thought to put down anything since our departure from the Azores, as it has been a very ordinary trip. But there was a worrisome occurrence today. I was looking over some charts in my quarters when I heard a clamor abovedecks and rushed to see what was the matter. Two men, Akers and Michaelson, were having a right row. Akers had a knife in his hand, and took a swipe at

Michaelson right before my eyes as the other men cheered him on. I demanded to know the meaning of all this, and Akers turned to me with wild eyes. Truly, I felt as though I were looking on the devil himself. With the knife in his hand, it was difficult to stand my ground. Still, I knew my duty as captain, and I did not move.

Michaelson accused Akers of stealing his knife.

Akers is a small man with dark hair and flashing eyes, and he hissed like a viper when he admitted that he did steal the knife. His long nose and furtive manner reminds one of vermin, and he crouched in a ratlike way as he reported, "Ee's been helpin' 'isself to extra rations in secret, ee 'as. So's I just made it a wee more difficult for 'im, didn' I?"

This aroused grumblings from the men. I felt their tension behind my back. It was true, I had decreased the rations for the past few days, as the winds have been light and we may be out to sea longer than expected. But this disobedience was a foul sign. I asked for a defense from Michaelson, who looked like an animal in a trap and acknowledged taking more than his share. He then sprang at Akers, who lashed out with the knife.

A bright red stripe appeared along the length of Michaelson's forearm, but he was the larger of the two, and he pressed forward with all of his weight until he was nearly crushing Akers against a barrel. He slammed Akers's hand against the barrel once, twice, all the while ignoring my command to stop. He kept smashing it until the knife finally fell from the crushed knuckles.

Akers reached for Michaelson's throat, but Michaelson had the superior strength. I thought for sure that Akers would be killed, but at that moment my first mate, Owen Moore, stepped forward and yanked Michaelson away. Akers stood up and made to lunge at Michaelson again, but two large deck hands stepped forward and caught his arms. Still, he struggled against them like a cat in a bag.

Moore looked at me. He's a tall man, with the blond hair of the Swedish, and eyes like the calm sea. He moves slowly, but with extreme firmness. He and the men hauled Akers and Michaelson belowdecks.

Around me, the hands were silent. I ordered them back to work and they went, albeit grumbling. I do not like this dawning mood among the men. Resistance and insubordination will not be tolerated on this ship. But I will have a talk with Moore to make sure that the punishment for Akers and Michaelson is swift and harsh.

If we are to be on the sea much longer, there will be greater sacrifices to be made. And resistance could spell mutiny.

July 14

39° 20′ N, 53° 03′ W

The waters have gone strangely calm. Nor does the air move. It is almost as if we are sailing on a sea of glass. I imagine we are like the waterbugs I've seen skimming over the surface of a still lake. Their long legs make only the slightest impression on the water. Here we are, like them, simply waiting for the wind to change.

Michaelson received seven lashes for his infraction, Akers five. Moore was efficient and professional, and I am grateful to have such a man as first mate. This was done in full view of the men. Michaelson cried out during his caning, but Akers made not a sound. He merely looked at me with those vermin eyes. His silence was as odd as the breathless wind, and truly sent a cold feeling into the pit of my stomach. Still, I dared not look away, as that would be seen as a sign of weakness among the men.

When it was over, Braithwaite jostled me slightly with his elbow as he passed and did not offer an apology. I gave him a dressing-down, but did not like the look in his eyes.

I sometimes feel the dark glances of the men as I pass by, and I fear they have still not forgotten what happened with Hawken. Their mistrust and anger linger.

But they would do well to remember that lesson. No one is important enough to imperil the entire ship.

No one.

July 16

39° 20′ N, 55° 45′ W

Still no wind. If we do not move soon, I will have to cut rations further. Perhaps we shall find a small island somewhere in which to refill our barrels of fresh water. But I do not wish to refresh the men's anger.

July 21

39° 20′ N, 59° 39′ W

We've gone to half rations. The men are both idle and tired, for there is little to do aboard a ship with no wind, and yet the idleness makes their bones weak.

July 23

40° 01′ N, 63° 52′ W

The sea is moving at last, and we've caught a fine breeze. I feel the spirits of the men lifting, like a dark curtain.

July 27

40° 40′ N, 65° 43′ W

There was a desperate knock at the door of my quarters this evening, and when I answered, there stood Moore, and Akers was with him. Akers was wild, shouting that we had to "save the girl." I looked to Moore for an explanation, but he said that he couldn't get Akers to make sense. Akers screeched that there was a girl in the water—that we had to save her. We rushed abovedecks and raced to the starboard side, where Akers had seen the girl in the light of the moon. But when we looked out, there was nothing but empty sea below a moonlit sky.

Akers scanned the waters, as if he expected the girl to reappear. Moore looked at me, and I knew that he and I had the same thought. We were miles from any known shore. What girl could be this far out to sea, all alone, no sign of another ship anywhere on the horizon? Akers was clearly mad. But we're a man short already, and I am loath to lock him up.

Perhaps I am making a grave error. Either way, I fear for the men.

July 29

41° 20´ N, 66° 52´ W

A banging at my chamber door startled me out of sleep. I was jolted from a vivid dream, and for a moment, I even forgot where I was. I'd dreamt that I was alone on the ship in the middle of the sea. The waves lapped like a cat's tongue at the side of the boat. Above me was blue sky, around me the wide waters. A feeling of dread stole over me like the coming of the night. I scanned the horizon, but perceived no threat. It was then that I noticed a tarpaulin at the foredeck. It appeared to be covering something, perhaps a barrel. I leaned forward to inspect it more closely, and the tarp lifted slightly, as if with a breath. Fear clutched at me, squeezing my lungs. It was with that feeling still upon me that I awoke.

The banging persisted, and someone let out an incoherent shout. In my disoriented state of mind, I leapt from the bed and rushed to the door. Outside was a horror—a haggard face stared at me with bulbous eyes, their whites exposed, like a vision from the grave. It was Akers. Moore was with him, as was Walters. They stood behind Akers, looking serious. Akers cried that "she dragged 'im down!" He then grabbed my arm and tried to force me from my chamber. Moore pinned Akers's arms behind his back and warned Akers of the consequences of his actions.

But Akers continued to screech, and he looked so frightened that I motioned for Moore to unhand him. Moore half dragged, half shoved Akers into my chambers and I motioned toward a seat. His face contorted as he struggled to control himself. I could see that he was in agony of an almost physical sort. Akers insisted that Michaelson had seen the girl, too.

I glanced at Moore and Walters, and Moore reported that Michaelson had disappeared. The watchman heard a splash, like someone falling overboard, and Moore found Akers abovedecks.

I stole a glance at Akers, who was squirming in his chair. I poured him a glass of stiff whiskey, and he drank it straight, gratefully. He closed his eyes and sat back, then held out the glass again. I hesitated, unwilling to part with it. It's fine stuff, a gift from a dear friend. But it was clear that I would never hear the story if I didn't make another offering. I poured another glass, and Akers downed it. He managed to collect himself somewhat, and finally continued his tale.

He said that the girl in the water sang to him in the voice of an angel. She spoke some strange language—perhaps it was the language of heaven, he didn't know. He said that every now and again, she would put her face into the water and her head would bob below the surface. But then she would appear again. After a time, she called to him and Michaelson. Akers feared that she was drowning. He started over the rail to save her.

At this point, I interrupted him, to ask how he planned to get her back to the ship. It is hard to describe the expression that came over Akers then. He looked simply shocked, as if I had risen from the dead to offer this query. He put his hands to his temples. He said that his head was full of fog. As if he had been under an enchantment. He shook his head twice, as if to clear the mists.

He said that he was about to climb over the rail when he head a splash and saw that Michaelson was swimming out to save the girl. He was no more than fifteen feet from the girl when she bobbed below the surface of the water again and disappeared. But there was something in the tilt of her head—she placed her face in the water right before she dropped beneath the surface. As if she was WATCHING for something. But before Akers could let out a shout of warning, Michaelson was dragged below. Akers said that Michaelson didn't even protest. "Ee sank like a stone and didn't come up again."

His voice had gone quiet by the end of the tale. He looked like a man overwhelmed by fear. I understood his emotions, for it had chilled my bones to hear his tale. There is no doubt about it—Akers has gone quite mad. He's killed Michaelson.

I told Moore to secure Akers in irons belowdecks for the remainder of the voyage.

Akers pleaded and cried, but Moore and Walters were already dragging him away.

I pray to God that we have no more trouble from him.

July 30
42° 20´ N, 68° 30´ W
Still a fine breath of wind.
Not a gale, but enough to fill the sheet. The

sails are puffed out now, like the chest of a proud father. And that is how I feel, indeed, as I walk the decks and I see the men hard at work securing the lines and running up the rigging.

I have taken to strolling the deck several times during the day and at night. This morning, Braithwaite was singing as he climbed the rigging to the crow's nest. It was a low, mournful tune, but it made me smile to hear it. The men were singing again.

Moore stood near the railing, looking out at the choppy sea. Some of the waves wore white, blown by the breeze.

I stood beside him, watching the blue sky as it paled to near white where it touched the horizon. There was nothing but sea in any direction. I noted that it made one feel as if one was alone in the world.

Moore noted that we aren't.

His words struck my ears like a blow, and I asked him for an explanation.

"Just that we've a whole crew, don't we? And a universe of fish below us, too, and God knows what else."

I did not like to hear those words, and I said so. Then Moore asked if I was certain we had done right by Akers. I asked if he had cause to doubt it. Moore said that Akers has gone quiet as a clam since he was shut down belowdecks, and is gentle with everyone. He said the men are curious why he is locked up, as we are three men down.

I protested that Akers is mad, and killed Michaelson. Besides, I told him that I feel as if the men have drawn a new breath, a deep sigh of relief, now that Akers is secured belowdecks.

Moore said that perhaps they would, if it weren't for Hawken.

I fear I lost my temper, then, and I boxed Moore's ear rather sharply. He looked at me—a look of shame and disgust. I felt it cling to me like warm candle wax. Or perhaps that was merely what I was feeling. I'd never struck one of my men before, and I didn't know what to say in such a situation. With much struggle, I managed to collect myself.

Moore was staring off at the horizon. He did not look at me, but said that he had overheard the men talking. They fear that Hawken cursed us. That when we left him behind, he placed a hex on the ship. The words spilled out and seemed to slip below the water like a leviathan.

Braithwaite's tune floated down to me. It sounded like a dirge.

Moore added that the sailors feel that this is a ship of death.

The cool wind blew across my face. Sailors are a superstitious lot. I knew this, even when I decided to pull up anchor while Hawken was still on the island. I should have known that the men's simple minds would turn this way.

Hawken had been out with a small party collecting firewood when he disappeared. Roberts said that he was there one moment, and the next—gone. Vanished.

We searched for three days while we laid up stores for the trip. There was fresh water on the island, and a strange large fruit with orange flesh. We'd collected many of them in barrels. Walters had even managed to catch some sort of pig with a spear. The flesh was gamey, but savory, all right, and the men had feasted well. But there was no merriment among them. I could tell that they were worried about their comrade.

But by the fourth day, when we had not found Hawken, I decided that we could not wait forever. Hawken was dead, I was sure of it, fallen off a cliff or attacked by a wild animal. The island had claimed him, and we had to move on. Our shipment of port and silk was expected, and I had been warned by my superiors that they would brook no delay.

And so, on the morning of the fifth day, we loaded the lifeboats and rowed back to the ship. The men were angry, I could see, but it was only Akers who protested. He insisted that Hawken would come back. But he didn't, and we had to leave.

We pulled up the sail and it filled taut, and I watched the shore recede as the ship started out onto the open sea. Just before it disappeared from view, I could have sworn that I saw a movement near the shore—a flash of red among the thick trees that grew at the edge of the island. But it disappeared.

I told no one.

I couldn't take the risk. I thought the crew

could mutiny if they thought Hawken might be alive. And I couldn't afford to be wrong, could I? Just as I couldn't afford to be wrong now.

I told Moore that I would not release Akers.

Moore nodded and gave me a salute, then turned to go.

A leader must be firm. That is the one lesson I have learned as captain of this ship. Doubt is the enemy. There is no room for it on this ship.

July 30

42° 22´ N, 69° 15´ W

Another hand—Iverson—has gone missing. And with Akers chained safely below.

No time to write my suspicions, as there is a noise outside my chamber.

Later

It was Moore. My God, but he looked like a madman when I came to the door. He was babbling something about the children, how we had to save the children. He dragged me abovedecks, but when he pointed over the port side, there was nothing but smooth sea, like a bolt of black silk beneath a silver moon.

He cried out that he saw them. I asked how many there were. He looked at me as if he didn't quite know who or what I was. His face appeared unshaven and the white flesh on his face seemed to sag, like a slack sail. His collar was undone and he looked altogether ragged, not like the creased and tidy first mate I'd known for years. It occurred to me that I hadn't noticed him becoming so unkempt, and I wondered how many other signs I'd missed from the rest of the crew. Had my own head been in a fog? What was the matter with me?

Finally, Moore said that there were seven of them. They were in two lines. Just their heads above the water, their long hair fanning around them like strips of seaweed. And they were singing. Sobbing, he said that he could still hear them. He tore at his hair, gnashing his teeth like a rabid animal.

I grabbed him by the shoulders and gave him a shake.

He cowered a little and looked up at me. His voice was a whimper as he repeated that he could still hear them.

The moon is on the wane, and the light was

weak. But still, I could see how pale Moore was. He looked like a feeble version of his former self, as if the Moore I had known had been locked away in a prison for years.

And now it has become clear that Moore has gone as mad as Akers. I am at a complete loss. How can I sleep? Moore might strangle me in my bed. I must protect the crew. But this madness seems to be spreading. Who knows who might be the next to fall victim?

We must make the rest of this journey quickly. I pray to God for fair breezes.

August 1

42° 25′ N, 69° 41′ W

The wind and sea have conspired against us. The sail is as limp and calm as a sheet on a featherbed. Only the men are restless. I feel their eyes on me as I walk the deck. They look haggard and tired. We have gone to four-hour shifts. That means they only rest four hours at a time, then they work four, and on half rations.

I do my best to keep up a good front. If they

sense weakness in me, I know that they could turn, like snarling animals.

August 2

42° 29′ N, 70° 02′ W

May God in heaven protect me, there is no one on this ship but myself and two madmen. I had convinced Moore to sleep in my quarters under the pretext that I wanted the protection. But while we slept—or, rather—while he slept, and I kept watch, four more hands were lost.

At dawn, I went abovedecks to see to the changing of the shift, but the deck was completely deserted. There was nothing but the creak of the sail and the sound of water lapping at the sides of the ship.

It was eerie, like a ship of ghosts.

I called for the men, but none answered me. I went belowdecks, and there was Akers, alone in a corner with his chains. He was humming the same mournful tune that I'd heard from Braithwaite days earlier. I asked Akers where the men were.

He replied that "the child had taken them." His face was completely affectless—it was as blank as the page on which I write. There was no fear in his eyes—there was no expression at all. It was as if the fear had devoured him, and left nothing. He predicted that the child would take us all.

When I returned to my quarters, Moore was gone. Where, I know not. There was no one to see me as I ran up the steps. I felt sick, like I needed to cast something from my guts.

I cannot sail this ship alone!

As I looked over the bow, I saw a small splash. Could it have been a head? Or was it just a jumping fish?

My God, this madness is affecting me now. I fear it won't be long. . . .

August 3

42° 29´ N, 70° 01´ W

Heaven help me—I've seen it. I know not whether I am mad—I think it is likely that I am. But I will describe here what I have seen. That thing on the water is no child. Perhaps it is a ghost, I know not. It is luminous—the reason the men could see her face in the light of the half moon is because she shines with a light of her own. As I stepped to the bow of the ship, she called to me. She sang, and it was with the voice of an angel—all the while dipping below the surface, as Akers had described. The music called to me, and I felt paralyzed. And yet I wasn't, for my feet were moving forward of their own accord. I was overwhelmed with a need to go to the child. My mind was infected with the desire to save her, although I knew the danger. She was calling me, and I WOULD go to her—it was as if I had become a river rushing forward with its own unknown force. I was at the edge of the ship, imagining the satiny feel of the cool water, and it seemed to me that it was like the lining of a coffin, and yet what struck me was not the fear of death, but the infinite rest, the comfort. But before I could take the final step, there was a horrible crash below. A moment later, Akers appeared abovedecks. His wrists were bloodied, and he trailed a thick chain that ended in screws and splinters. He had pulled the chains from the wall. When he saw the child, he let out a cry and leaped from the side of the ship. And then, something—I know not what it was—pulled him down. The ghost child tilted her head and smiled at me, and I would have followed Akers, but in that moment, she disappeared.

Slipped below the surface like an eel.

I know now what I must do. I must lash the helm in place, so that we keep a straight course. Then I will lock myself belowdecks, so that I cannot jump overboard. I will pray that we run aground while I am still living. If not, please give my love to my wife and son.

I hope that I may yet make it home, and back to sanity.

Will flipped through the pages that followed, but they were all blank. At the back of the journal was tucked a brittle old newspaper clipping, yellowed with age. A corner broke off as Will unfolded it, gently flattening it against the page. He let his palms rest against the book for an extra moment, hoping they would stop shaking.

He looked down at the newspaper clipping.

Ship Runs Aground Near Walfang

The *Eliza Thomas* was found yesterday near the port of Walfang, run aground on a sandbar. It was half sunk, and au-

> thorities fear that it will take a great effort to remove it from its mooring place at the edge of the bay. The ship left port four months ago from Portugal with eight hands, plus captain and first mate, and was presumably on its return voyage. The hull was loaded with port, silk, and fine silver, all unmolested. And yet there was not a soul aboard. There were signs of a peculiar struggle in the men's main quarters, as if something had been ripped from a wall, but aside from that, the ship was pristine. A captain's log has been found, and authorities hope that it will help reveal the cause of the missing crew. . . .

Will stopped reading. He didn't need to know more—he knew already that the log raised more questions than it answered.

Is that what Asia is? One of those—things? *Those things in the water . . .*

He looked out the window, toward the horizon, at the unseen ocean beyond. Will imagined that he could hear their subtle whisper. The endless pounding and sucking of the waves. Suddenly the ocean itself seemed like a devouring creature. He'd grown up near the water—he'd spent endless hours in the waves, splashing and playing. He'd never been a sand castle maker—maybe that was why he'd never paid attention to the sea's destructive power. But over the past year, he'd begun to have trouble seeing it in any other light.

Will crossed the room quickly. He opened his bottom drawer and pulled out the flute. The instrument was roughly the length of his forearm, and he shivered as a thought occurred to him. Was this—could it be—a human bone? Was this the remnant of some frightened sailor, dragged to the bottom of the sea?

That's stupid, Will told himself. But—what about Asia's voice, the one that had stopped Jason in his tracks? What about that strange, melancholy song that Gretchen had been humming recently? Did that mean anything?

Will shuddered. He wished more than ever that he could talk to Tim. Will's brother had always known what to do. He was smart and practical. Somehow, if Tim had just been there to tell Will that he was acting crazy, Will knew that he would have believed it. Then he could just stop looking for answers. And if Tim had thought that Will *wasn't* crazy, well, that would have helped, too. But there was no one else he could really trust with this information. He couldn't tell Angus. And he didn't want to tell Gretchen—she had enough problems.

There was a hole in the world where his brother used to be.

Chapter Ten

Seekrieger Chantey (Traditional)

Death is like a river,
And rivers are our home.
Home, home!
Yes, death is like the river
Styx, flowing over bone.
We flow just like the water,
And fall just like a wave.
Wave, wave!
Yes, we flow like water,
And bring you to your grave.
As slowly dripping water
Can wear away a stone,
Stone, stone!
Seekriegers wait a thousand years,
And take men, one by one.

When Gretchen stepped outside that night, there was a figure on her doorstep. She took a quick step backward in surprise and fear—for a moment, she didn't recognize the broad, square shoulders, the shaggy, shoulder-length hair streaked with blond. She realized who it was a moment before he turned to look at her. In profile, she could see the boy he used to be—the long, straight nose, peeling slightly with the usual summer burn, the fine, high slant of a cheekbone, the familiar denim blue of his eye. And then she saw his full face, which had grown chiseled and taut over the past year, and the familiar scar that tore from forehead to cheekbone. Gretchen realized that Will was taller than she was, even though he was standing a step below her.

He held her eyes for a moment, and Gretchen dared to imagine that he was thinking the same thoughts she was. And then he opened his lips and said, "What do you know about mermaids?"

The question was so unexpected—so far from her own thoughts—that it rocketed her back to the present with the speed and weight of a falling meteor. It crashed into her mind, and she laughed. "Da seaweed is always greenah," Gretchen sang in a Jamaican accent, just like the spunky crab in the Disney movie, "in somebody else's lake. You t'ink about goin' up dere, but—"

"I'm serious." Will's face was unusually stony, and the words withered on Gretchen's lips.

"You're serious?" she repeated. She wanted to add, *About mermaids?* but Will's expression was grave.

"Have you ever heard any local stories?"

"Local? No." She shook her head. "No . . ."

"You just thought of something." Will stepped up to the porch. He looked down at her. "What?"

"Stop reading my mind." A flash of annoyance shot through Gretchen.

"It's not your mind I can read—it's your face." He put a warm hand on her shoulder. "Please tell me."

"Well, they aren't exactly *mermaid* tales. But I was

just remembering the stories Sally used to tell." Sally had been Gretchen's nanny when she was young. She was a local woman whose family had lived in Walfang for generations.

"Sally." Will nodded, remembering. "Is that why you were always afraid of the bay?"

Gretchen shrugged. "Probably."

"Okay. So tell me."

"She just never wanted me to go down to the water, that's all. She claimed the sea witch could get me."

"What sea witch?"

"She would drag children to her undersea cave. Sally used to say that the witch could control the weather and waves, and she'd get angry and irritable when the days got shorter, at the end of the summer. Anyway, I always thought she was just making it up to scare me, so that we wouldn't have to go down to the beach. Sally never liked going to the beach over here. She'd never take me swimming in the bay." Gretchen remembered how Sally's wrinkled face would set into a firm mask of resistance at the mention of the bay. She would drive twenty minutes to take Gretchen to the public beach, but she would not take her down to water that was only a five-minute walk away. Sally had dark skin and a heart-shaped face with pronounced cheekbones. Her eyes were almond shaped and dark under thick brows. But she had frosted blond hair streaked with gray, which she wore in a long braid down her back. She had been adamant about the dangers from the witch. "Deadly Sea Woman," Sally had called her.

Will seemed to absorb this. "Can I talk to her?"

"I think she moved away. To live with her daughter in Georgia, or someplace. I have no idea where she is."

"Can I borrow your computer?"

"Sure."

They walked into the living room, where Johnny was plucking a melody on his guitar. It was almost as old as he was—Johnny always composed on the very first guitar he'd ever owned. He never used it for concerts, but he considered it his "creative machine."

Will waved and Johnny nodded, but he didn't put down the guitar or give any other acknowledgment that he'd seen Will. He simply went on, playing the melody in his head, filling the house with eerie music. A strange look crossed Will's face then, and Gretchen wished that she could read his expression as easily as he seemed to read hers.

Gretchen led the way up to her room. It was just the usual chaos—rumpled white quilt halfheartedly straightened across the bed, books and magazines everywhere, a sketchbook open on the floor revealing a study of a wing with hyperarticulated feathers and musculature. And beside it, a painting. *Maybe he won't notice,* Gretchen thought.

"Where did you get that?" Will asked instantly.

Gretchen felt her face turn red. "It appeared."

"It *appeared*?"

"Seriously, Will, it just turned up on my bed yesterday."

"You have to call the police."

"Won't the Miller think I stole it?"

Will thought a moment. "I'll call Angus," he said. "His uncle Barry can get this sorted out."

Gretchen nodded. "Would you?" She cast a wary glance at the painting. "The thing gives me the creeps. Who would leave it here? And why?"

"Maybe it's some sort of message," Will said slowly.

Gretchen grimaced. "Next time, they can just shoot me a text."

"I'll call Angus later," Will promised. Gretchen flopped onto the bed and watched as Will settled into the chair and the screen leaped to life.

Immediately the chat she'd been having online with her mother appeared. Will's hand paused over the mouse, and she knew that he'd spotted it. But he didn't mention it. Instead, he started typing into a search engine. He came up with several pages on sea witches and Long Island.

"What are you finding?"

Will scanned a page. "Not much more than what you told me," he admitted. "Sea Woman," he added, half to himself. "She was a giant." He shrugged. "Not too helpful."

Gretchen tucked her legs beneath her and leaned against a pillow. "Why do you want to know all of this?"

Will turned to look at her. "How's your sleep-walking?"

"It's okay. I mean, I'm still doing it. Dad has to lock me in at night, which is really annoying. But yesterday I woke up curled up at the foot of the door, so I guess it's a good idea." She gave a little laugh.

"How do you get out?"

"I call Dad on his cell phone. Wake him up, usually. Then he sets me free."

"What would you do if there was a fire?"

"Die, I guess."

"At least you have a plan."

"I could climb out the window." There was a maple tree that grew close to the house. The branches were near enough to the window that Gretchen could climb down it if she needed to. In fact, she had done that once or twice. Not that she'd ever had much need to sneak out of the house with her father as her primary caretaker. Gretchen could simply stroll out the front door whenever she felt like it. But when her mother had been living with them, it was a different story.

Guitar notes wafted up to them. It was a sad melody, slow and strangely familiar. Gretchen hummed along, her eyes half closed.

After a moment, she became aware that Will was watching her. "What?"

"You know the tune?"

"I guess."

"Isn't Johnny making it up?"

Gretchen realized that she had no explanation for this. "Maybe it sounds like something else."

"Maybe," Will said. But he had a look on his face that Gretchen knew well. It was the same look he wore when he had something to say but wasn't saying it. "Maybe, but maybe not—right?"

"Stop reading my mind."

"It's your face I'm reading."

Will smiled a dry little smile and stood up. "I've got to get going."

"Where?"

"Downtown."

"Just wait a few minutes," Gretchen said as she slid her feet into a pair of flip-flops. "I'll come with you."

Will didn't really want her with him. He needed to talk to Asia, not Gretchen. But how was he supposed to say no? He was starting to worry about Gretchen. The sleepwalking wasn't a good sign. And he didn't know what to make of the correspondence he'd seen between Gretchen and her mother. Gretchen's mother lived in France and they didn't talk much.Will remembered her. She was petite, almost child-sized, with blond hair and very fine features. She was slender and had an elegant bearing. She never wore fancy clothes or even makeup, but a beautiful smell always hung around her, which Will realized now must have been expensive perfume. She was not a warm person, and Will had always been half afraid of her, even though she had never spoken a sharp word to him.

One summer, Gretchen and Johnny had come out during August. Yvonne wasn't with them. When Will asked where Gretchen's mother was, she replied in the sagacious way of an eleven-year-old, "She doesn't live with us anymore." As if she were a stray cat that had moved on. Gretchen had hardly ever mentioned Yvonne after that. Sometimes Will even forgot that Gretchen had a mother at all.

"Why are we here?" Gretchen asked as she parked the Gremlin in front of the upscale vintage store that sold ostrich leather boots for $300 and hand-beaded gowns for close to $1,000. For used clothes! Will couldn't believe it the first time he'd gone in there. The prices had appalled him. It was closed now, the usual porch display gathered up and dragged inside to keep thieves from stealing the valuable cast-offs.

"We're here because I need to talk to somebody."

"Somebody specific? Or just anybody?"

"Somebody specific."

"Somebody we might find at a diner?"

Will looked at her sharply. Gretchen had turned to face him. She was leaning back against the car door in an elaborately casual pose, as if she were seated in a comfortable easy chair. Yet her body looked tense.

"What makes you say that?" Will asked.

"I don't know. But I'm right—right?"

"Yeah, I need to talk to Asia."

"Why?"

Will sighed. "I'm not really sure yet." He yanked the door handle and stepped out onto the brick walkway. Gretchen scrambled after him, and they started up the street toward the diner. When they turned the corner, they found a very weird scene. There was a crowd clustered in front of Sebastian's, an upscale bar. For a moment Will assumed that everyone was there for the club scene, but then he realized that they weren't gathered outside the door. They were gathered near the curb. And they were looking up—into a large purple-leafed maple at the curb, illuminated in an eerie glow by the light of a street lamp.

"Oh, Jesus," Gretchen breathed. "It's that crazy kid."

A branch shook, and Will spotted Kirk clinging to the trunk with one arm and gesturing wildly with the other. "We're all born angels!" Kirk cried as they stepped forward. "But we lose the wings. We lose the wings, and how can we fly when we don't know our own depths?" Suddenly his eyes lit on Gretchen. "Did you get the picture? Did you see it?"

Will looked at Gretchen, who was standing stock-still.

"Did you see the truth in it? You can hear them, too. I know you're one who can hear them as well as I can." Kirk's eyes were wild, and for a moment Will feared that he might leap out of the tree, like an animal. He put a protective arm around Gretchen, and Kirk let out a scream. "Don't touch her!"

A siren wailed as Will steered Gretchen away from the scene. A police car pulled up, casting red and blue shadows across faces. A uniformed officer stepped out of the car, along with Kirk's sister, Adelaide. She was a stern-faced young woman with the perfectly coiffed hair of a professional stylist. Adelaide looked like she wanted to apologize to everyone personally and then go home and quietly die of shame. Will cast a sympathetic look over his shoulder. Kirk was shouting something else about angels now, and his voice had reached a fevered pitch. Will felt as if something had crawled into his stomach and was hastily constructing a nest there. He felt sick and shaky. *What's happening to that kid?*

Will could feel Gretchen trembling beneath his arm. "What was he talking about?" Will asked.

"I have no idea," Gretchen said. She had always been the world's worst liar, but Will didn't press her. "I'm going in here," she announced suddenly as they neared a candy store. "I need some chocolate." She took the top step and looked back over her shoulder, long blond hair flying. "You coming?"

"I'll wait out here," Will said.

Gretchen disappeared inside, and Will leaned against the glass. He folded his arms across his chest and settled in for a long wait. Gretchen could be a bit of a candy freak, and she liked to get one each of many different kinds. She always took her time selecting things, and it drove Will crazy. Besides, candy on an empty stomach would make him sick. He was already feeling pretty borderline.

And that was when he spotted her. Asia was across the street, watching Adelaide coax Kirk down from the tree. He stepped forward to say her name, but she noticed him then. She turned and began walking away.

"Hey," Will called as he jogged after her. "Hey!"

Asia stopped, but she didn't turn around. Will caught up to her. He looked deeply into her eyes for a long moment. She cocked her head.

"What are you looking for?" Asia asked.

"What are you?"

She scoffed. "What do you think I am?" Her voice was a challenge.

"That's what I'm trying to figure out."

Asia pushed past him. He hesitated. That conversation hadn't gone according to plan. He knew that he wasn't handling this situation properly, but he had no idea how he was supposed to be handling it. He wasn't even sure what the situation *was*. "Asia, wait." Will reached out and grabbed her arm, and it sent a shock wave up his arm. He cried out in pain.

Asia stood stock-still as Will gaped at her.

"I'm sorry," she said at last. She reached out for him, but he drew back from her touch. "It won't hurt," she promised, and she gave his arm a brisk massage. Slowly it came back to life.

"What the hell was that?"

"It's just something I can do . . . when I feel threatened. I don't always do it on purpose."

"Like an electric eel or something?"

Asia sighed. "Will, I have a great deal to explain to you," she said.

"Um, yeah," Will agreed. "Look, I know you're a mermaid . . . seekrieger . . . thing, so why don't you just tell me what's going on? All I want is a little clarity."

She laughed.

"What's so funny?"

"Nothing's funny," she said at last. "Nothing."

Will waited as she stared at the stars overhead.

"I have a story to tell you," Asia said at last. Her voice was like a thin vapor, a fine mist dissolving on the air. "It's a long story."

"Will it clear anything up? Or will it just leave my head feeling like it's going to explode?"

"Both, maybe," Asia admitted.

Will touched her hair, brushing it away from her face. It trailed over his fingers like black ink.

"Just tell me."

"Yes, but not here," she said.

"Then where?"

"Meet me at the library tomorrow morning."

"I can't. I have to go to work."

"Then meet me there tomorrow evening. Six?"

"Okay, but you'll be there, right? I don't want you ditching me."

Laughter sparkled in her eyes. "You haven't figured it out yet?"

"What?"

"I'm not like you humans, Will. I can't lie. That's why I don't talk very much." She stood and brushed the sand from her long maroon dress. "You'll hear the truth, but I can't promise that you'll like it."

The next morning, Will and his father ate breakfast in their usual tense silence. When Mr. Archer was finished, he took his plate to the sink and headed toward the door. He nearly ran into Angus, who was on his way up the steps. "Hey, Mr. Archer."

Will's father nodded at him and kept walking.

"Wow, your dad's cheery this morning," Angus said as he scrambled inside and stuffed his long legs under the table in the seat next to Will's. "Dude, are you going to finish that?" He pointed to Will's scone.

"Yes."

Unfazed, Angus plucked the remnants of Will's

father's toast from his plate and started smearing pear jam on it. "Your mom makes the best stuff."

"Why are you here?"

"What's wrong with everyone this morning?" Angus demanded. "What happened to 'Hey, Angus, great to see you'?"

"Great to see you. Why are you here?"

"Something freaky happened. I kind of wanted to tell Gretchen, but I'm not sure how."

"What?"

"You remember Jason Detenber?"

"That asshole," Will said.

"Don't say that too loud," Angus advised.

"Why not?"

"He's dead."

"What?" Will felt sick. His throat constricted, making it hard to breathe.

"Well, he's disappeared," Angus admitted. "My guess is he's fish food."

"What makes you say that?"

"Remember that white jacket he had? I saw it at the police station. Only it wasn't too white anymore, if you know what I mean." He lifted his eyebrows meaningfully at Will. "It was in an evidence bag. But nobody was saying anything. Not *anything*. I mean, guys who can't help talking were suddenly like clams. They didn't even want to say hi to me. I think my uncle scared them silent. But Jason's family is rich. The truth is going to have to come out, sooner or later."

The image of Jason and Asia on the bridge flashed into Will's mind. The way he had moved toward her threateningly. The way she'd twisted backward and flipped into the water. Jason's horror. Asia's watchful face, her eyes upturned from the water. Had she marked Jason for death at that very moment? Had he sealed his own fate, like the sailors in the journal?

But Will didn't say any of this to Angus.

"Gretchen's gonna freak," Angus noted.

"Yeah," Will agreed.

"You wanna tell her?" Angus asked hopefully.

The knot in Will's stomach tightened at the thought of facing Gretchen with news like that. "No, I really don't," he admitted.

"But you will," Angus said.

"Do I have a choice?"

"You're a good man," Angus told him.

"Not really."

Angus sighed. "Okay. I mean, maybe he's okay. It's not like anyone really knows what happened, right?"

Just one person, Will thought. But what he said was, "Right."

"Oh, hey—and guess who's in rehab?" Angus tipped back in his chair, stretching his long legs under the table.

"Is this person a celebrity?"

"Just a local one. Kirk Worstler."

"Seriously? Where'd they get the money?"

"Word is Adelaide finally called the grandparents. They've got him locked up in some fancy place in Hampton Bays." Angus stood up and helped himself to some fresh coffee.

"Listen, speaking of Kirk, it seems that he left a

gift in Gretchen's room." Will explained about the painting.

"Oh, shit. Okay, I'll call Uncle Barry. He'll get it taken care of." Angus shook his head. "That poor kid. I'll bet the Miller won't even press charges."

"Thanks, man. I owe you."

Angus held out his fist for a pound. "We gotta stick together."

"Sure."

"Sure? Just—you know, 'sure'? Man, how about some enthusiasm?"

Will managed a smile. "We gotta stick together," he said.

When Johnny came to the door, he told Will that Gretchen was upstairs in her room and said Will should head on up. Will took the steps slowly, dreading the moment when he would have to deliver the news. But when he pushed her door open gently, he saw that the room was empty. The normal chaos was unusually tidy—the bed was made and the large painting was spread out over it. Will stared down at the image of the fierce bird-women on the rocks in the distance. Their expression made his heart splutter, starting and stopping in frantic motion. He completely understood why it gave Gretchen the creeps. He wondered what Kirk had been thinking when he left it for her. He was glad the kid was finally in rehab. For Kirk's own safety—and everyone else's.

A movement caught Will's eye, and he looked out of Gretchen's window. There was the green bluff, and beyond it, the blue-gray sea. A figure in green stood at the edge of the bluff, long blond hair sweeping down her back. Gretchen was looking out to sea like a sailor's wife, waiting for her husband's safe return.

Will hurried down the stairs and out the door. His legs ached as he climbed the bluff. A lonely seagull cried overhead. Finally Gretchen came into view, and Will slowed as he got near her. He didn't want to frighten her.

Gretchen didn't turn around. "Jason's dead," she said. Her voice was heavy, and it was weary.

"How did you—?"

"Do you think that there's anything to what Kirk was saying?" Gretchen asked. She gazed out at the distant horizon, a faraway look on her face. "About angels?"

"I don't know," Will admitted.

"I wonder what it's like."

"What?"

"Being dead."

Will shrugged. "It's like being asleep."

"Sleep without dreams." A gentle breeze lifted a lock of her hair. She had added colorful strands to the blond. With the blue and green streaks, she looked like a storybook mermaid.

"Yeah."

"How do you know?" Gretchen asked.

"I don't. It's just what I think."

"I don't think that's what it's like," Gretchen said. She seemed on the verge of saying something else, as if the words were like bits of mist assembling into clouds in her mind. There was a long beat of silence as Will waited for her to go on. "Sometimes I think I can hear them," she said at last.

"Dead people?"

She shook her head. "I don't know."

Will studied her profile, noticing the dark circles under her eyes, how pale her skin seemed beneath the light kiss of sun across her nose. He'd always thought of her as walking sunshine, but now the light within her seemed dim. Very dim. "Have you been sleeping?" he asked her.

She laughed, and the sound was brittle on the wind. "Stupid," she muttered.

"What?"

"Forget it."

"No, wait—what did I say? What was stupid?"

"Not you, me," Gretchen snapped. "I should have known."

"Known what?"

"Known that if I told you the truth, you'd think I was nuts." Gretchen narrowed her eyes at him.

"I don't think you're nuts," Will told her. He reached out and pressed her hand. Her skin was soft beneath his own.

She looked down at their intertwined fingers. Her hair hung over her face, half obscuring it.

"I'm just afraid," Will said.

Gretchen's eyes met his. It was strange to see that gaze, at once so familiar and so unfamiliar. There were flecks of green in those blue eyes. It was as if you could see the whole world in Gretchen's irises. Will wondered if he'd ever noticed that before.

He didn't remember.

She placed her cheek against his chest, as if she was listening to the beat of his heart. Will placed an awkward arm around her shoulder, wondering what to say, what to do. "I'm afraid, too," Gretchen told him.

"Jason might be okay. Just because they haven't found a body—"

"They never found Tim's body."

Will was rocked with the truth of this. He was speechless.

Gretchen pulled back to look up into his face. "I—I'm sorry," she sputtered. "I don't know what's wrong with—"

"No—" He held up his hand. "It's true. Sometimes, I think part of me is still waiting for him to come back."

"We could wait forever."

"I know."

They stood there like that for a while, both staring out over the water, flat as a blank page. "It's so strange," Gretchen said after a moment. "I was sleepwalking again last night. Here. At the edge of the water. Do you think that means something?"

"Out here? I thought Johnny was locking you in."

"I must have climbed down the maple tree," Gretchen said.

"So what are you going to do? Nail the window shut?" Will was kidding, but Gretchen didn't laugh.

She shook her head. "I don't know."

"Gretchen," Will said slowly, "who told you about Jason?"

"Asia did."

"She did? She called?"

"She came by."

"Is she still here?"

Gretchen's eyes filled with tears, which mystified Will. "I—I'm sorry," he stammered. "I just need to ask her—"

Gretchen shook her head. "It's okay." She ran her fingers along the rims of her eyes, then wiped the tears on her loose green jersey dress. "Sorry. I'm just . . . everything is making me cry today." Tears welled in her eyes again, and Will pulled her into a hug.

"We're going to get through this," Will said.

Gretchen nodded her head against his chest. "I know," she said. "I just wish I knew what was on the other side."

Chapter Eleven

From the Walfang Gazette
Happy 375th Birthday, Walfang!

Saturday marks the 375th anniversary of the founding of Walfang, which was—along with Boston, Salem, and New York City—one of the eastern seaboard's most important port towns during colonial times. There will be a parade and concert to celebrate the founding. . . .

The library was a small white Greek revival building that had stood at the center of town for two hundred years. Two incongruously thick columns guarded either side of the periwinkle-blue doors, holding up the tiny roof with Atlas-like drama. It could have been the library in any small town, except that the names of the authors who were scheduled to perform readings were the kind of names you saw in New York City, for a fee. Every author in the Hamptons wanted to appear there, both to show how "community-oriented" they were and to prove that they belonged in the famous-authors club.

The warm, slightly sweet smell of old books haunted the place. Gretchen used to drag Will here on weekday afternoons. They'd to go to the children's section, at the back, where she'd poke around among the novels while he checked out nonfiction. Will had always liked biographies, which made Gretchen roll her eyes. "Real life is boring," she'd say. But not the real lives he read about. He'd gone through a period in which he read everything he could about Ernest Shackleton, an explorer whose ship became stranded in Arctic ice in 1915. He liked stories about survival.

The librarian didn't look up from her computer screen as Will shut the door gently behind him. The library was nearly empty. A pouty boy with pale blond hair sat in a corner while his slim mother chatted on a cell phone. He reached for a book from the top shelf, and the mother's gold bangles jangled as she snapped at him and frowned. The kid scowled. He looked freshly scrubbed, as if he were on his way to a photo shoot. Will felt sorry for him.

Asia was on the other side of the library, at a table near the windows. An open book was spread out before her, but she wasn't reading. She was looking out the window. Will slid into the chair across from hers.

"I shouldn't have left him on the bridge," Asia said. Her face was dark as the sea beneath a coming storm.

She didn't need to explain whom she meant. Will knew she was talking about Jason.

"Did you have anything to do with what happened?" Will asked.

"Not directly."

"Not *directly*?" Will looked at her carefully. "Or no?"

She continued to stare out the window. "There are beaches, far from here, where, if you kick the sand at night, it sends up tiny green sparks. It's just a phosphorescent microorganism. Plankton, that's all. But it looks like starlight at the edge of the water."

"Am I supposed to know what the hell you're talking about?" Will replied. He wrestled his voice into a hoarse whisper rather than a scream. "How about some clarity? Yes or no, Asia—did you kill Jason?"

Asia looked at him then with those crystalline green eyes. "No."

"Did you kill my brother?" The words spilled out of him, sharp as tacks.

Asia's green eyes softened. "No, Will," she said gently. "No."

Will's tense body relaxed ever so slightly. He believed her. *Maybe I shouldn't,* he thought, *but I do.*

Asia smiled sadly, and she pushed the book toward him. "Were you ever made to read this?" Asia asked.

Will flipped to the cover. It was a worn cloth-bound edition, the dust jacket lost long ago. Gold letters were nestled into the faded navy cover. *The Odyssey,* it read.

"Freshman year," Will said. "I don't remember much about it. Didn't they gouge out somebody's eye?"

A smile played at the corners of Asia's lips. "The Cyclops, yes."

"And didn't Ulysses kill all his wives' boyfriends?"

"They weren't her boyfriends," Asia corrected. "They just wanted to marry her for her money."

"I guess I remember the bloody parts," Will admitted.

Asia pointed to a passage near the bottom of the page. "Do you remember this?"

Will scanned the page.

"Read it out loud," Asia commanded.

"'First you will come to the Sirens who enchant all who come near them.'" Will hesitated. The words seemed to crawl over his skin, tickling up memories from the journal he'd read. He looked up at Asia, who was scowling out the window.

"Go on," she whispered.

"'If any one unwarily draws in too close and hears the singing of the Sirens, his wife and children will never welcome him home again, for they sit in a green field and warble him to death with the sweetness of their song. There is a great heap of dead men's bones lying all around, with the flesh still rotting off them.'" Will looked at her closely. "So what exactly is a Siren?"

"Siren, mermaid, naiad, Oceanid . . . there are many names," Asia said. "Many names for the same thing."

"That doesn't answer my question."

"What we are? Who knows?"

"You're not human?"

Asia laughed. "No."

Will sat back in his chair. He looked at her carefully—her perfect skin, her luminous eyes, her silken hair. She did look almost unreal. Still, hearing it from her own lips made him feel a little dizzy. It wasn't that he was surprised. It was more like he was relieved. *At least I'm not crazy. Or at least I'm not the* only *crazy one.* "So . . ."

Asia lifted an eyebrow.

"Do you have . . ." He shook his head, searching for the word.

"A fin?" she prompted.

"Yeah. I guess."

"No. No, I don't turn into a fish or a bird. No, it doesn't feel as if I'm walking on glass every time I take a step on land. No, I didn't give my voice to a sea witch."

"So what's different about you? Do you have superpowers?"

Asia looked out the window. "We don't die. If you consider that a superpower."

"Don't *you*?"

Asia's expression turned a shade darker. "Not really."

"You don't die, ever?" Will had a hard time grasping that. He never used to think about death, but now it seemed like he thought about it all the time. He couldn't really imagine what it would be like to never have to worry about that.

"Not that I know of. Perhaps we just have a long life span. Perhaps we're immortal. None of us has ever died of natural causes, at least not that I know of. But we can be killed."

"So—wait a minute. How old—"

Asia toyed with the frayed edge of the old book. "I remember many things," she said. Her eyes met Will's. "Many of these things."

"That stuff in the book? That—"

"We have lived among humans for a long time. Some of us, like Calypso, even married among them."

"*This* Calypso?" Will pointed to the book.

"The very same."

Will thought that over, fighting the damp, clammy feeling that was slowly creeping up the back of his neck. He held his head in his hands and suppressed the desire to run screaming from the library.

"It's hard to hear, I know," Asia said.

"It's hard to *believe.*"

Asia blew out a sigh. "Well do I know it."

Silence pulsed between them like a living thing.

Will tried to collect his thoughts. The persistent sense of unreality that had hung around him ever since Tim died seemed to press in further. *If this is a nightmare, I wish I would just wake up,* he thought. But he didn't wake up. And so, with a deep breath, he pressed on. "You knew Calypso?"

"She was my sister," Asia explained. "We all are sisters."

"Then who are the Joyces?"

"Who?" Asia's expression seemed genuinely blank.

"You live in their house?" Will prompted.

"Oh." Asia bit her lip, looked away. "Will, this town is full of empty houses. Every year I find a seaside town, and then find a place to live. If the owners return, I simply move on to another house."

"What will you do it they come back and find you?"

"I can usually tell when the owners are coming back."

"So the Joyces aren't your family?"

"I've never met them."

"So, no family. And there aren't any mer-guys?"

Asia laughed. "No."

"So how do you . . ." Will waved his hands, and Asia lifted her eyebrows.

"Reproduce?"

"Yeah."

"We don't. That is, we can have children . . . with humans. In the usual way." She smiled wryly. "But those children are human, not our kind. None of us remembers our births, obviously, as you don't remember yours. We've simply always been. But there are no new mermaids. When the last of us die . . ." Asia shrugged.

"Maybe there used to be mermen," Will said.

"That's what I think. Perhaps something killed them off. But I don't know." She breathed a gentle sigh. "You have no idea how frustrating it is to have no idea where you came from." She traced her fingers in loops over the top of the table. "And you have no idea how terrifying it is to consider a death that's so final. There won't be any family left."

"You're the last?"

"Not exactly."

"You're going to explain that?"

"I'll try."

Will decided to let that go for a moment. "All right, so—do you have any other special powers? Can you breathe underwater? Are you like Aquaman or something?" He tried to laugh, but it came out sounding strangled.

Asia turned her head and lifted her long black hair. There, behind her ear, were three black gash marks, like a dark tattoo. They quivered slightly.

"Gills," Will whispered. He had to swallow hard to keep from vomiting.

Asia nodded. "I don't choose to live in the water. But I could. Calypso has."

Will shook his head, dumbfounded. It took him a moment to gather his thoughts enough to ask, "And what else?"

"We're very strong," Asia admitted.

"Should we arm-wrestle?" Will joked.

"Only if you want me to rip your arm off." Her green eyes glittered, and Will went cold. "Not that I would, of course," Asia added.

"Uh, thanks, I guess."

The mermaid chuckled.

But a new thought had occurred to Will. "So, that night—the cliff—"

"Yes."

"Can you fly?"

Asia shook her head. "No. We can climb. And jump."

"Jump," Will repeated. "So—wait—"

"I was near the water already that night. I'd heard something. . . ."

Will raised an eyebrow.

"You didn't, by any chance, play that flute of yours?"

Will cast back in his memory. Guernsey, barking. Looking out the window. "Yeah, I did."

Asia nodded. "That flute . . . it's what we use to call each other."

A chill swept through Will's body. "Do you know why my brother would have had one?"

"Are you sure your brother *did* have one?"

"I just—" Will suddenly remembered that the flute had been found on Tim's boat . . . but that didn't mean it was actually Tim's. "So why did you sell yours?"

"I had used it for the last time."

Will could tell that he wasn't going to get a more specific answer. At least, not yet. "Okay. So that night . . ."

"I was by the water, and I heard you calling for Gretchen. I saw you struggle at the edge. And I saw you fall, so I jumped toward you. Instead of falling straight down onto the rocks, you got knocked off course and fell onto the sand."

"Some jump."

Asia smiled slowly and reached a hand across the table in a feline stretch. "I'll show you sometime."

"Okay." Will wasn't really sure he wanted that. "So—wait. You're immortal . . . but can you get hurt? You know, injured?"

"We don't die of natural causes, Will. But we can be injured, yes. We can even be killed."

"How?"

"Fire." A shudder ran through her body, and Will remembered that she had said her sister died in a fire.

"What happened?" Will asked.

Asia pressed her palm flat against the book, as if her body were absorbing its words. "After the Trojan War, Ulysses became lost on the sea. We had helped the Greeks in their fight, and many of my kind had fallen. We returned to our homes weary, and most of us foreswore violence. But there were a few for whom battle had kindled a bloodlust in their veins. Ulysses sailed to Calypso's island. Calypso loved Ulysses, and she thought that he loved her. He lived with her many years, before he finally decided to return to his wife, his home. He left with promises to return, but these promises were broken. As you know, my kind cannot lie, and we do not understand when others lie to us. Calypso waited patiently for Ulysses to return. Ten long years she waited, until finally she realized that he did not plan to return at all."

"And she was pissed."

"Please don't interrupt."

"Sorry." Will grimaced.

"But yes, she was pissed, as you put it. She sailed after him, and found him safely at home, with his wife and grown son, Telemachus. And there were two new children—a son and a daughter. Rage washed over Calypso, and she killed Ulysses. She killed the children. The grown son escaped, as did the wife, Penelope. But Calypso left their entire village in ruins before she left.

"But the story didn't end there. Haunted by what had happened to his family, Telemachus swore vengeance on Calypso and all of our kind. Penelope was a wealthy woman, and very powerful. Her mother, Periboea, was one of us, and she knew our weakness.

With her help and Ulysses's name, Telemachus found many followers. They set sail to hunt us down. When they came to Calypso's island, they took many of us, although they did not capture her. Those were very dark years." Asia closed her eyes.

"They knew our islands, and sought us out. And so many of us took to the sea. The rage in Calypso's heart had only grown more furious and treacherous. She swore vengeance on all men with dark hearts."

"But how could she know who—?"

"I'm getting to that, if you would stop interrupting. We have a sixth sense."

"You can read minds?"

"No. Not minds—hearts. Emotions. Not perfectly, but we sense anger, fear, pain, despair. We don't necessarily know what is causing those emotions, and often they are blended with other emotions, which makes them difficult to understand. But the powerful emotions call to us. . . . Calypso began to defend herself against rogue sailors by sensing their intentions. And then she would attack."

Will considered the journal. The sailors had been fearful, angry, wretched over the loss of Hawken. Then Akers had unnerved them. Had those dark fears, that fury, called the seekriegers to them?

"For many years, Calypso and her mermaids have lived near the bottom of the ocean. Over time, their eyes grew larger. Their skin grew luminous. They feed on fish and other things from the sea—but they hunt men."

"Just men?"

"Humans," Asia corrected herself. "But sailors are—were—usually men so most often those are their victims."

"You keep saying 'they.'"

"I'm not like them." Asia grimaced slightly, like one in pain, and Will suspected that she might not be telling the whole truth. She wasn't lying—not exactly. He believed her when she said she couldn't. But she could leave things out. "Calypso and her band—those are your seekriegers," Asia told him. "I'm not with them. We're the same kind, but we don't want the same things. I've always chosen to live on land, for example. And for a long time I tried to stay away from humans, whereas they seek them out."

"But there's more to the story," Will prompted.

"Much more." Asia looked wistful. "Telemachus came for me and my sister, Melia, but we escaped him and his band. We decided that we could not stay in that part of the world. We swam toward a land that we knew was more secluded—where the natives were friendlier to our kind. There we stayed—alone—for ages. Time passed; hundreds of years, then thousands. It was a peaceful life, but lonely. When we missed the company of humans, we visited the natives, who welcomed us. Still, a thousand years is not forever. New people began to arrive, and although they looked different from Telemachus and spoke differently, we felt the same anger in them. But we lived on an island far from the new settlements, and we did not swim near them. We watched the great boats with their many white sails float by like swans.

"One evening, there was a storm out at sea. The gray sky was lit with cracks of lightning. The waves raged against the rocks. Rain lashed at the ocean as if it were an enemy.

"Our kind are often drawn to the violent sea—sailors used to call a hurricane a 'siren's storm.' I don't know why we go to the water in a tempest. Perhaps we're seeking the calm beneath the waves. I found Melia at the water's edge, watching as a ship slowly climbed a steep wave. Our eyes are keen, and we saw it crest the top, then plunge. The next wave was larger. The wave curled over the ship, which listed to the side. The wave crashed with the force of a mountain, and I know we both felt it—the fear of the men, the panic as their ship splintered apart. We were far, but the terror carried out over the water.

"Melia bounded into the water. Her leap became a dive, and she disappeared beneath the waves. I dove in after her.

"We surfaced near the men. One old man was clinging to a large piece of driftwood. When he spotted Melia, the panic in his eyes turned to something animal. Melia tried to reach for him, but he kicked and flailed, and finally she had to let him go.

"A young boy with huge, frightened eyes looked up at me. He was paddling like a dog, and I could tell that he could not keep it up much longer. I grabbed him, while Melia reached for a man who was floating facedown nearby. At first, I thought he was dead, but she yanked back his fair hair. His eyes fluttered open, then closed again.

"The next wave was rising, so I placed the boy on my back and started toward our island. But the old man was swimming toward Melia, shouting. He reached for her arm, but grabbed instead a fistful of her hair.

"I cried out to her, but a wave dashed down, driving the old man and the mast forward. As the wave crashed, the mast knocked Melia on the head, and I saw her go down. The old man was thrown wide. A moment later, the wave came for us. I dove and swam until the rocks of the beach scraped my fingers.

"Our kind swims fast as dolphins. Still, the boy tumbled from my back as I stepped onto the beach. His face was pale, almost blue. He was still for a moment, and then he choked, writhing, and vomited seawater—much more than I'd thought a small boy like that could hold. I stood over him as he shivered and cried and vomited more, but I was facing the sea. The wave had erased the ship. And it had erased all signs of Melia.

"I cared for the boy, and he adored me. I caught fish for him, and fed him such fruits as grew on the island. I sheltered him and treated him with the medicine I knew. He was weak for a long time. He carried a small knife in his pocket. He had not lost it in the storm, and with it, he carved small animals for me from pieces of driftwood. He carved a cat, and a mouse. A fish. A snake. My favorite, though, was a small bird. These he presented to me in silence, while his large dark eyes looked up at me in eagerness. He tried to communicate with me, which is how I first learned English."

"Sorry to interrupt, but—what year was this?"

"Years had no meaning to me then," Asia answered. "It was over three hundred years ago."

Air escaped from Will's lungs in a whoosh. For some reason, that number—three hundred—made Asia seem more ancient than the stories of the *Odyssey* had. It was more tangible. *Three hundred years ago.* He felt sick.

Asia cocked her head, and he knew that she felt the change in his emotions.

"Is it hard, to have such a long life?"

Asia closed her eyes, then opened them slowly. "I don't know. I've never known anything different."

"Right."

"Shall I go on?"

"Just give me a minute."

"We can stop," Asia offered.

Across the library, the mother argued with her child, warning him that it was time to leave. The world spun on, full of the mundane, full of mystery. It was hard to fit together. Will couldn't sort it out.

"No," Will said finally. "We can't stop."

"All right." Her hands were folded, and she looked down at them. "Where was I? Oh, yes. The boy. I cared for him for several weeks. Then the weeks became months. He taught me English, and I began to teach him my language. He seemed enchanted with me, and wanted to spend all his time with me. He was becoming more and more like me every day. When I heard him singing one of our songs in his sleep, I knew that it was time to return him to his people. But I had grown fond of him, and I did not want to merely abandon him at the port. I needed to observe things, find where he might live.

"I came ashore at night and stole from a drying line the sort of clothes I would need to fit in. It was early November, but the air had turned bearably warm. Still, the clothes were stiff with frost as I beat them out and put them on. Then I waited. The next morning, I prowled about the market stalls, overhearing bits of conversations. There was a strange energy in the air—everyone was talking about an upcoming trial. The town was awash in dark feeling—there was fear, and excitement, and righteousness, and anger.

"I was pretending to pick over a pile of potatoes when I caught a movement out of the corner of my eye. Something about the gesture seemed familiar to me. And when I turned, I saw Melia at the next stall. She was dressed in a gray gown, with her red hair tied up beneath a simple gray cap. Still, there was no way to hide the beauty of her face.

"She must have felt my gaze, for she turned. When she saw me . . . well, I can't describe what came over her face at that moment. It was shock, really. Her eyes stayed on mine, but they were far away, as if she had entered a dream. I felt her confusion, and then, slowly, the confusion slipped away, like steam disappearing on the air. Her eyes returned to me then, and I saw that she knew who I was—and that she hadn't known a moment earlier.

"A pretty young woman was at Melia's side. She was dressed as Melia was—in simple gray, with a full skirt and a clean white apron. She was slight and fair-haired, with large blue eyes and a sweet, heart-shaped face. The girl looked at me inquiringly, and placed a hand on Melia's arm, and this seemed to recall Melia to herself. Melia spoke a word to the girl, and she nodded. She smiled at me, then made her way through the market as Melia came toward me.

"I told her that we should leave that very night. She could return to the island with me. We both knew that it wasn't safe for her here. Our kind has never been safe among yours, not for long. I wanted to simply grab Melia and flee—take her far away from those people. I could smell the rage in the air, like drifting smoke. All I knew of them was that they would have killed me if they had known what I was.

"But Melia refused to leave. She had fallen in love with the sailor she had rescued, James Newkirk, and he loved her. She said that she would rather live a short while with him and lose him than live forever without him. She had to take whatever time was granted to her. It didn't matter if it was only thirty years, or fifty, or five. It didn't matter if it was a moment. She loved him. It was the beginning and the end, for her.

"I asked her to remember the times we were hunted. She said that she did remember. And so I left. It was the last time I ever saw her.

"When I returned to my island, my boy was shivering in his sleep on the floor of my shallow cave. He heard me stir, and the look of relief on his face when he saw me sent a strange feeling through me. What was it? Gratitude? Happiness? Perhaps it was a form of love.

"The fire had gone out, so—very, very cautiously—I lit it, and he warmed himself. I despised the fire, but the boy needed it. He had caught a slight cold, and I busied myself with caring for him. I doted on him for several weeks, long after he was well. I suppose I told myself that he was too weak to go back to his kind. But I think I really didn't want to let him go.

"I decided to keep him with me through the winter. In the spring it would be easier for him to find work, or even a family to take him in. And so I kept him safe, and fed him, and sang him to sleep at night.

"In the spring, I helped him build a boat. We loaded it with food and waited until the waters were calm. Then I hauled it out over the breakers and into the wild sea. I had braided a rope, and I fastened that between my waist and the boat. Then I hauled the boat to the port. The boy had outgrown his clothes by then—they were nothing more than rags, anyway—so I stole clothing for both myself and him.

"I had in my mind a vague thought that perhaps Melia could find a home for my boy, but I knew not where to find her. I searched all day, and combed the market, but she was nowhere to be found. Finally, I asked an old sailor if he knew James Newkirk, and he said aye. He directed me to a handsome house on a tree-lined street. All of the homes were large and square—this was the row where the sea captains lived. I asked the boy to wait at the foot of the stairs while I lifted the large brass knocker.

"I did not recognize the face of the woman who answered the door, and I asked to see James.

"She said that she was his sister, Elizabeth. Then I realized that she was the young woman I'd seen with Melia in the market months before. Her face was so altered—it seemed gray with age, and there were lines around the bright blue eyes. But the same sweetness lingered in her expression. I told her that I was looking for Melia.

"She let out a little noise then—part sigh, part gasp. I felt her fear, her horror, her despair.

"Melia had been arrested on suspicion of witchcraft. Arrested . . . and tried. And found guilty.

"Not that it was much of a trial. Elizabeth and James, of course, testified on her behalf. But there was too much evidence against her. There was her mysterious, sudden appearance in town. Her lack of memory. Her unnatural beauty. Her red hair. And Melia did not even have family to speak for her.

"She was sentenced to burn.

"Melia had been dead for months, and I hadn't even known it. When I heard this news, I felt sick. I thought I would vomit, but Elizabeth put out an arm to steady me. She said that she had a letter from Melia. She had slipped it to Elizabeth in secret, when she had come to visit her before the trial began. Melia had instructed Elizabeth to give it to me if she ever saw me again.

"I opened the letter. In it, Melia described her love for James and her fear of the stake. 'My dearest Asia,' it read, 'please care for James. He has done everything he could to save me, and I fear that his anguish makes him desperate. If he were to go to sea with these feelings, you and I both know what could happen to him.'

"I remember reading that and feeling fear pierce my heart. Elizabeth told me that James's craft had departed ten days before, en route to South America.

"I flew down the stairs so quickly that I nearly crashed into my boy. His expression made me stop and turn. Elizabeth was still standing in the doorway, watching me. I asked Elizabeth to care for him, and then I left. I had to get to the sea.

"The ocean is a vast place. Even you, who live at its edge, cannot comprehend its immensity. But I knew something of the sea lanes—something of the routes. And I knew that James's pain would carry far, very far.

"I knew that my own felt as wide as the acres of water before me.

"For three days, I swam. I caught up to them off the coast of Georgia. The water had gone eerily calm, and I knew—I knew that Calypso was nearby. But I did not see her, nor any of her band. I stayed close to the ship and waited. For two more days the ship sailed south.

"Sometimes I saw James stand near the port bow. I would have recognized him even without his captain's uniform, for he looked very much like Elizabeth. He had the same fair hair and blue eyes, but where her expression was all sweetness and innocence, his was full of wisdom and compassion, and sadness.

"When the winds changed, they changed suddenly. And on the breeze, I heard the song—Calypso's song.

It was so beautiful and melancholy, even I felt drawn to it. And how could the sailors resist such a song? They didn't even realize that they were hearing it. The music entered their minds like a thought, and soon they were sailing off course.

"For a while I wasn't sure of her intent. But I knew that two thousand years had not made Calypso weary of vengeance. If anything, it had only fed her bloodlust. I think that her original betrayal—Ulysses, Telemachus, Penelope—had been all but forgotten. She had become nothing more than a receptacle for anger, for blood. She killed because she loved the killing.

"She drew the sailors away for half a day more. The sun was beginning to set, sending wide ribbons of orange and purple across the horizon. The sea was calm, but not unusually so. We had moved south enough to enter beautiful weather. The water was warm, the air mild against my face.

"The ship was a three-masted schooner, tall and lovely. The figurehead was a mermaid, carved and painted, with bare breasts and long golden hair. The vessel sliced through the water smoothly, sending a line of white foam in its wake.

"The ship wasn't far off course. Calypso didn't seem to be drawing them into foul weather, or toward any island that I knew of. I watched the ship, puzzled. I decided to swim alongside it for a while.

"Then I saw what she intended. She was drawing them toward a group of rocks. They were below the surface of the sea, and invisible to the sailors. But I could see them.

"There wasn't much that I could do. It was too late—the ship was bearing down on the rocks, and in a matter of moments the boulders' jagged edges had torn a wide hole in the starboard hull.

"It groaned and heaved, and sailors struggled to man the lifeboats. Others simply jumped overboard as the ship rolled over onto its side like an old dog.

"In a moment, the water was swarming with seekriegers. The sea was thick with bodies as Calypso and her band descended on the sailors. They wore ragged clothing made from the hides of seals and other sea creatures, which made them look animal and fierce. The men who jumped overboard did not come back up to the surface. Soon the blue water ran with red.

"One lifeboat was overturned, then another. James had been directing men into the boats, but when he saw what was happening, he stopped. He had a pistol, and he started firing it into the water, at the seekriegers. A few other men grabbed firearms, but most had none, or else were already struggling in the water.

"I swam as close as I dared, but I feared he might shoot me. He would not know that I was there to help him. How could he?

"A seekrieger clawed her way up the side of the boat, and he took aim at her. She staggered back under the blast and dropped into the water.

"But another seekrieger was behind that one. I recognized her by her silver hair and violet eyes. It was Calypso. She reached for James, and he fired again—but the chamber was empty.

"I dove toward them and met them as Calypso dragged him into the water. He looked around in horror as his men were slaughtered, and I could feel his guilt—these were his men, and he had not saved them.

"I called out to Calypso, and she turned in surprise.

"She smiled a slow, languid smile, revealing teeth that had been sharpened to shark points. Her large eyes blinked at me in the twilight. It had been many years, but she knew me. She called my name.

"James looked at me closely, as if he recognized the name. I wondered if Melia had spoken of me.

"I told Calypso that I had come for James, and she looked at him with new interest, as if he were a jewel that she hadn't realized she had.

"'What will you give me in exchange for this life?' she asked.

"I told her that I would give her anything.

"She studied him for another moment, smiling her strange shark smile. I thought that she would kill him then, bite into his neck or tear out his heart. But to my surprise, she released him.

"I grabbed him, held him as he struggled. He was strong, but not strong enough. I subdued him.

"'You will give me whatever I ask,' she said to me.

"Around us, the sea had grown quiet. Here and there, among the bloody water, dark fins had begun to appear. Smelling blood, the sharks had come. I saw a few of Calypso's followers. All of them had sharpened teeth and large eyes. Their skin was luminous in the darkening light.

"I asked Calypso what she wanted, and she replied that she did not yet know. 'I will call to you,' she said.

"I can't describe the feeling that overcame me then. I feared for the future—for what she might ask. I was swimming in a warm sea of blood. Calypso drew her dark lips back, revealing those hideous teeth. I felt something brush my leg—a shark. I knew that it would not dare to bother me . . . it was James that it wanted.

"Calypso just smiled. She knew as well as I did that it wasn't possible for one of us to break a promise. If we did, we faced a sort of soul death. We would not die, but we would have no more intellect. We'd become nothing more than a fish in the ocean, with no self-consciousness. A sort of zombie, I suppose, is what you would call it. I looked around. The other seekriegers had circled us, and I felt their bloodlust like it was my own. I could not fight all of them. And even if I tried, they would kill James.

"And in my heart, I had promised Melia that I would protect him. The moment I read her letter, I'd made the promise.

"So I took him.

"We traveled slowly. I had learned from my experience with the boy. I could not simply carry a human underwater with me. When we reached landfall, I built a boat, and I managed to tug him back to the closest port, which was Charleston. From there, he planned to contact his employers and tell them that the ship had run aground and the cargo was lost. Before I left him, I extracted a promise from him. I asked him to care for my boy. He said that he would. Even though I believed him, I still checked up on them once in a while. Indeed, James did take care of my boy, raising him as his own son. He retired from a life of the sea, and instead entered the military. He never married. I think he was the kind of man who could marry only once. And he had married Melia in his heart, if not before a judge or a priest.

"He was like us in that way. He could not break a promise."

Chapter Twelve

Song of the Sirens, from the Odyssey, *Book XII*

> No one ever sailed past us without staying to hear the enchanting sweetness of our song—and he who listens will go on his way not only charmed, but wiser, for we know all the ills that the gods laid upon the Argives and Trojans before Troy, and can tell you everything that is going to happen over the whole world.

Gravel crunched outside as cars sped past the little town library. An apologetic woman with a drooping face approached their table tentatively.

"I'm sorry, but I wanted to let you know that the library will be closing in half an hour." Her voice was a half whisper that sounded like a flute playing softly. She touched her glasses and flashed a self-conscious smile at Asia.

Will had noticed that about Asia—men wanted to catch her eye, of course, but women did, too. It was as if they wanted her approval.

Asia stood, her legs uncurling gracefully from beneath the wooden library table. "We're leaving," she announced. And she looked at Will.

Will didn't have the strength to argue, so he followed her.

Night had fallen, and the tall iron street lamps glowed yellow overhead as they stepped onto the sidewalk. They started away from the town. Will was glad. He felt wrung out, like an orange that's been juiced. An empty rind.

For a long time, there was only the sound of their footsteps and the rush of cars as they passed by. It was Will who broke the silence.

"So why are you here?"

"Calypso finally called to me. And I returned her call."

"And then you sold the flute."

"I have no more need to contact my sisters. And no wish to do so."

"What did she ask for?"

The question hung in the darkness for a moment.

"She asked me to deliver someone to her," Asia said finally.

"Deliver someone?" Will went cold. "You mean kill them?"

Asia put a hand on his arm. "I would never kill someone, Will."

Will shook off her grip. "Don't bullshit me, okay? That's just a technicality. If you hand someone over to those lunatics . . . So who did you deliver—Jason?"

"I haven't delivered anyone," Asia replied.

"Yet," Will snapped.

Asia sighed. "Yes."

"So—who's it going to be? What innocent person are you going to snatch off the street?" He gestured to the shopping district around them.

Asia shook her head. "Calypso has an enemy. Someone who has hunted her over the ages. This enemy disappeared for a while. But a year ago she reappeared."

"A siren?" Will asked.

"No. Nor human, either. The Burning One."

Will digested this information. "So why don't you just team up with Calypso's enemy and fight?"

Asia shook her head. "I can't, Will. If I break my promise . . ."

"So you didn't have anything to do with my brother's death?" Will asked.

"Will, I don't know what happened to your brother," Asia said. "I can guess, but I wasn't there."

"But *they* were—right? That's why the flute was there?"

"That is my assumption."

"And what about Jason?"

Asia sighed a delicate, lacy breath. "The seekriegers are here, waiting. It isn't safe—not for anyone with as much anger as Jason. They had already taken one, just a few weeks earlier."

Will felt this answer rather than heard it. The words made him tremble. Asia put a hand on his arm and said, "It's all right."

"Yeah." He laughed bitterly. "And by 'all right,' do you mean 'completely fucked up'?"

Asia winced. "All I can tell you is that once I fulfill my promise, they should depart."

"So why don't you do it, then?"

Asia looked at him for a long time, and he read the

pain in her eyes. "I suppose you could say that I am weak," she said finally.

Will ran his hands over his face. "Does Kirk Worstler know what you are?"

"I think so."

"Why? How?"

Asia shook her head. "I don't know."

"How can you do it?" Will's voice was almost a whisper.

Asia did not look at him. "I have no choice."

"There's always a choice."

Asia looked into his eyes. "Not every story has a happy ending, Will," she told him.

"Have you ever told anyone what you are?" Will asked.

"A human? No."

"So—why are you trusting me?"

"You already knew half the truth, and yet I sensed no danger from you. Besides, I know how it feels to lose someone. I know how badly you want answers. . . ."

Will placed a hand against his face, feeling the scar beneath his fingertips. "Why didn't Calypso kill me?"

Asia shook her head. "That is not for me to say."

Will laughed, but it was a bitter sound. "It's the only question I care about."

"I know, Will. I understand completely. And I wish that I could help you," The sadness in her voice was like a heavy weight—like an anchor dropping deep into the sea. Will could almost feel the heft of it. "But I don't have the answer."

Chapter Thirteen

From the Walfang Gazette
Court to Hear Dispute Between Neighbors

Millicent Halliwell, of Walfang, claims that her next-door neighbors have been keeping her awake with loud music. "I've heard it as late as three in the morning," Ms. Halliwell claims. "It's so loud that nothing blocks it out. I've tried earplugs, white noise, everything."

Her neighbors, Bruce and Daniella Narsburg, claim that they haven't been playing music late at night, and weren't even in town one of the evenings in question. "She called the cops on us," Mr. Narsburg told the *Gazette.* "But they didn't hear any music. This is just harassment, pure and simple." The Narsburgs have filed a separate suit. . . .

Will felt the rumble of the motorcycle in his whole body. The heavy vibrations shook him, rattling his bones as he sped down the black ribbon of road. His mind was still spinning from everything Asia had told him, and the noise and motion felt soothing to him. It felt normal—mortal.

Will's single headlight picked up a motion, and he swerved to avoid hitting the thing that had staggered into the road.

It threw up an arm and recoiled, and Will—too late—slammed on the brakes. The motorcycle shuddered, skidding to a stop. Will let it tumble onto its side behind him as he raced toward the man in the road. Will ripped off his helmet and dropped to his knees beside the limp form, which had fallen face-first onto the asphalt.

Gingerly Will turned the figure over.

"Oh my God." His voice was a strangled murmur when he caught sight of the person's face. He was young—a teenager—and pale. His eyes were huge and dark, his pupils dilated to the width of his irises. The whites of his eyes stood out in the darkness.

He looked up at Will with those wild eyes, and his face seemed to register something. He opened his cracked lips to release a strangled voice. "I know you," the boy whispered.

"Jesus Christ!" Will lifted the boy's head into the crook of his arm. "Kirk?"

Kirk laughed then, but it was a laugh without humor. "They've come for her." He grabbed Will by the collar, smearing the blue and white cotton of Will's shirt with blood. "The bay holds no fear. The fury must awake! Now is the time—they're waiting!"

Will struggled to free himself from Kirk's grip, but the crazy kid wasn't letting go. *What's he doing here? Isn't he supposed to be in Hampton Bays?*

Will looked down at Kirk's feet. He wasn't wearing shoes. His feet were bloody.

Kirk's teeth were gritted. "I've called to them." He

spat the words rather than said them. "They're waiting! I hear them!"

"What?"

But Kirk choked. He coughed, spitting up blood, and released Will from his iron grasp. He fell back then, knocking his head nastily against the pavement.

"Kirk?" Will hauled him back into his arms. "Kirk?"

But Kirk had passed out.

Will looked over at his bike. He wasn't sure he could get Kirk to the hospital that way. Instead he pulled out his cell phone.

What is it with Kirk Worstler? Will wondered as he dialed 911. *Why does he always need me to save his life?*

"Is he awake? Is he talking?" Angus slid into the soft chair beside Will in the hospital waiting room, talking a mile a minute. "Dude, tell me what he said—this is crazy."

Will put his hand to his head. "What the hell are you doing here?"

"Getting the scoop, man, what else?"

"But how did you even know—"

"Uncle Barry let me borrow a police scanner." Angus stood up and took a few steps toward the ER. "Is he—" Then he caught sight of some movement behind a curtain, and took off.

Will reluctantly hauled himself out of the comfortable chair. It was a beautiful hospital, made plush for the wealthy summer people who hurt themselves in a fishing accident or while slicing a bagel. Everything in the Walfang hospital was nicer than it needed to be.

Will wandered down the hallway, admiring the clean white walls adorned with black-and-white nature photos. But there was no way to make the beeping machines and medical equipment look elegant. The doctors and nurses in their blue scrubs, too, seemed like ugly afterthoughts in a pristine architectural concept.

Kirk was lying on a white bed half hidden by a gray curtain, with Angus hovering over him.

"How many, do you think?" Angus asked. "One? More than one?"

Kirk looked blank. "I don't remember." His voice was hoarse, as if he had just spent a week in the desert. A mauve plastic pitcher sat by the bedside, next to a stack of plastic cups.

"Look, try to remember. If there's some kind of gang—"

"This isn't the Crips and the Bloods, Angus." Will poured some water into a cup and handed it to Kirk, who took it, gulping madly. "It's Walfang. We have cows. Kirk's just torn up because he dragged himself from one end of the island to the other."

"Thanks," Kirk said when he had finished, handing the cup back to Will.

"Are you the interviewee?" Angus asked.

"What's happening?" Kirk asked. It was strange to hear him sounding so lucid—as if the drugs had worn off and he'd come back to himself, finally. He had a small voice, almost like a child's, and it made Will feel protective.

"Nothing. Just . . . don't worry about it," Will told him. "Angus, leave him alone."

"Look, I'm just doing my job," Angus said. "Is it wrong to want to get to the bottom of the story?"

"Actually, the doctors said there's nothing wrong with me," Kirk said. He looked down at himself. He was wearing a pale blue and white hospital gown. "They said—" His sentence was interrupted by the appearance of Kirk's sister. "Adelaide?"

"Doctors can't find anything wrong with you, except for scraped-up feet and some glass in your arm," Kirk's sister told him. "They say I can take you home." She didn't look particularly excited at the prospect. She tossed a pair of clean jeans and a folded T-shirt onto the end of the bed. "Put those on, and we'll get out of here." At that moment she seemed to notice Angus for the first time. "What the hell are you doing here?"

Angus looked offended. "Why does everyone keep asking me that?"

"Look, my brother isn't talking to you."

"What if he has something to say?" Angus asked.

"He doesn't." Adelaide flashed Kirk a stern glance. Kirk seemed to shrink a little under the glare, like a turtle retreating into its shell.

"Come on, Angus, let's get out of here." Will tugged at his friend's sleeve, and Angus flashed Adelaide one last glare before following his friend out the door.

They were silent as they stepped outside under the bright lights that illuminated the parking lot. Will felt the anger coursing through him, burning up, like a scrap of paper that flares, then turns to ash in a matter of moments. Angus pressed a button on his keychain, and a black BMW chirped in response.

"Where's your car?" Will asked.

"Dad's asleep," Angus replied. "I figured he wouldn't mind."

"You mean notice."

"That's what I said." Angus grinned.

"Okay." Will decided that it was easier not to argue. "I'll see you, man," he said as Angus yanked open the car door.

Angus leaned his weight against the top of the door. "Hey, Will," he called.

Will turned back. "Yeah?"

"Did he say anything to you?" Angus asked. "When you found him?"

"No," Will told him.

Angus nodded. "Poor kid. I don't know if we'll ever find out the full story behind Mr. Newkirk Alexander Worstler. Beyond the fact that he's completely nuts, I mean. Well—"

"Wait, what?" The wheels of Will's mind were spinning like tires on wet ice.

"I said he's nuts."

"No—you said . . . what did you call him?"

Angus shrugged. "Newkirk? That's his name. Must be a family name, I guess. Newkirk." He rolled his eyes. "With a name like that, no wonder he's crazy."

Will shook his head. “Family name . . .” Newkirk. As in James Newkirk. Could Kirk be related to the captain in Asia's story? But she'd said that James had never married again. Then Will suddenly remembered, *But he had a son. An adopted son. The boy Asia saved.*

The boy who understood her language. *He was becoming more like me every day,* Asia had said.

Will turned back. He started toward the hospital at a dead trot.

“Hey,” Angus called. “Hey, Will!”

Will ignored him. He had to talk to Kirk.

When he raced back into the room, Adelaide was helping Kirk out of his bed. Will's eye fell on a familiar shape on the bedside table, and his heart stopped. “Where did you get that?”

Kirk looked over at the flute. “I . . . I don't know.” But his face had turned white.

“Did you—were you in my room?” Will's voice was practically a scream.

“Hey, back off,” Adelaide told him.

“I don't know where it came from,” Kirk insisted, his face registering confusion. “I . . . maybe . . .” He put a hand to his forehead. “Where do you . . . do you live near the bay?”

“Just take it and get out of here,” Adelaide snapped. “Nobody cares about your stupid flute, asshole.”

“You didn't play it,” Will said.

A machine beeped, the only sound in the room.

“Tell me you didn't play it!” Will said.

Kirk shook his head, but he looked unsure.

Oh, God. Did Kirk call those hell beasts in from the water?

Suddenly Kirk's words came back to him like a horn through fog. *The fury must awake!*

Awake.

Will's eyes darted to the wall. It was long past midnight. *Gretchen,* he thought. If Gretchen sleepwalked while those things were in the bay . . .

Will turned and slammed into Angus, who was just coming through the door. "Dude!" Angus cried. Will stumbled, recovered.

And he ran.

Chapter Fourteen

From the Walfang Gazette
Yacht Ventures Into Bay, Causes Gas Spill

The *Penelope,* a yacht owned by fashion designer Newell Orlost, ran aground on a sandbar in Walfang Bay this afternoon. Unfortunately, her reserve tank of gasoline was ruptured in the accident, causing a sizeable fuel spill in the bay. Hazmat workers should be on the scene later tomorrow.

"Any time we see a spill of this nature, there is always a threat to wildlife," said Martin Olvides, professor of . . .

Guernsey was barking at the gate as Will roared up on his motorcycle. She went crazy when she saw him, leaping and lunging at the pickets.

Will unlatched the gate and reached for Guernsey's collar, but the dog pushed past him. She bolted toward the fields, her thirteen-year-old legs remembering their puppy speed. She led him across the yard, past the flowers now dim in the darkness, past the black sheep nestled in clean hay under their shelter. The dog blasted out into the field.

Will ran down the narrow row of corn after her. The stalks grew high overhead, blocking his view. They whispered past his ears, tearing at his arms, but he kept running. It was like a labyrinth with only one way out—forward.

Suddenly he broke through the vegetation, and the soil quickly turned to a mucky silt and sand. He stopped short. Guernsey was standing at the bay's edge, barking.

And Gretchen was in the water.

Her white nightgown billowed around her as she waded into the still, smooth bay. The water was already at her waist.

The moon hung like a jewel in the sky, pouring light down onto the bay. It was easy for Will to see the heads—the group of faces—in an arc facing Gretchen.

His bones felt hollow, hollow as a flute, or the barrel of a gun. He was light, without weight, without power. Those faces—lovely and strange, with eyes like stars and teeth like daggers, hungry mouths—struck a primal fear in him. It rooted him to the ground, kept him captive while their voices drew Gretchen forward.

Sound filled the air, coiling like ropes around Will's ankles, around Gretchen's mind. The faces bobbed and watched as Gretchen slogged her way forward. One, two, they disappeared into the water, then resurfaced. Suddenly, Gretchen slipped below the surface. It was quick, as if she'd fallen into a hole—one moment she was there, a figure as white as the reflection of the moon, and the next, she was gone.

Will could only watch, helpless and immobile, as the music held him captive. Will tried to cry out, but he couldn't find his voice. Even Guernsey grew quiet. She crouched on her belly, whimpering.

Will couldn't be certain if their song had words. If it did, they were words he didn't understand. Yet images flashed into his mind—clear images. A sudden flash of Tim's face. The fear, the strange underwater scream. They were both there. A woman with hair like starlight looked at Will. She smiled, revealing small, sharp teeth. Then she tore into Tim's neck with those teeth. . . .

Blood curled through the water like smoke on air.

Will struck out, and a laser of pain slashed across his face. He felt as if his cheek had split open. He prepared for the teeth to tear into his flesh, ripping it like scissors, but instead someone grabbed his arms, dragged him away, hauled him—a dead weight—back onboard the boat.

Eyes fluttering, Will saw a face leaning over him. Blue eyes, long wet pale hair hanging in thick ropes. Behind him, at the edge of the water, the sail on Tim's boat had caught fire and blazed into the night like a vision of God. Then the image started to fade, slipping away. . . .

The arc of faces dipped into the water, and suddenly the music that held him went silent. The trance lifted slowly, and Will remembered where he was. He was at the edge of the bay . . . at the edge of the bay, where he had gone after Gretchen. . . .

"Gretchen!" Will shouted as he plunged forward, his thick boots chopping into the water like heavy axes.

Water churned suddenly, and Gretchen's face appeared. She fought her way to the surface, but a hand reached out to pull her back down. She managed a single, strangled scream before she disappeared again.

He took five steps, then stopped. He didn't know where to go. Ripples spread out in wide rings, then melted into the water, erasing evidence of their existence. The bay was smooth as glass.

"Gretchen," Will cried, scanning the water for any sign. Any sign.

There was none.

But still he stood there, his muscles tensed, ready to fight, ready to dive in after her.

Silence.

Then, with the suddenness of a lightning bolt, the water broke open with a deafening scream. A figure blasted through the surface, blood pouring from its face. It took Will a moment to realize that the figure wasn't Gretchen—it was one of the seekriegers. A fierce cut was lashed across her face, and blood poured into her eyes, blinding her.

The water roiled and shattered as another seekrieger blasted out. A hand reached up and caught the creature, and in the next moment Asia appeared.

"Oh my God," Will whispered as Asia grasped the seekrieger's hair. She twisted her neck with a jerk, and sent her back screaming into the water. Another seekrieger appeared behind Asia, but she knocked her elbow into the mermaid's face, sending her flying backward. And then she dove.

Will held his breath.

The ripples had barely disappeared from the surface of the water when Asia, with Gretchen in her arms, leaped from the water and landed near the cornfield. Will dragged through the mud, racing to join them as Asia let Gretchen spill from her arms to the ground.

Gretchen coughed, then rolled over to vomit seawater onto the sand. Will fell to his knees beside her as she choked and sputtered, shivering in her drenched nightgown. Guernsey came over and licked Gretchen's face. Gretchen moaned.

"She'll be all right," Asia said quietly.

Will stared at her. "How can you say that?"

She looked out across the bay. "They're still waiting."

"Who are you delivering, Asia?" Will demanded.

She remained silent.

"Who is it?" Will screamed.

Asia looked down at Gretchen. "The Burning One."

"Gretchen? Are you talking about Gretchen?"

"The person you know as Gretchen, yes. She's the one Calypso has been seeking."

"You're making a mistake. She isn't—"

"Not yet, Will. But soon."

Will threw a protective arm across Gretchen. "You've got the wrong person!"

Asia shook her head. "No."

Will lunged toward her. Asia opened her mouth, and a single note fell out. It blasted against Will like a cannonball, dropping him to the ground.

Will panted, trying to regain his breath. "Why did you save her, then? If you're just going to hand her over?"

Asia looked down at Gretchen. "I'm no executioner," she said.

"So what are you going to do?" Will asked.

The seekrieger with the hair like silver sang out, seeming to call to Asia. Out in the bay, the seekriegers shrieked and sang. "Calypso is waiting. She'll be paid, one way or another."

"Just walk away," Will urged her.

"You know that's impossible." Asia's voice was melancholy, but there was no mistaking the core of steel at the center of the words.

Gretchen let out a low moan.

"What are you going to do?" Will asked.

"The only thing left," Asia told him. Turning, she raced into the bay with a speed that almost defied his vision.

"Asia!" he shouted, but a splash, then spreading ripples were the only sign of her.

The seekriegers let out an inhuman shriek and plunged after her. Will could see nothing for a long, sickening moment. Then Asia surfaced, facing Calypso.

The sirens faced one another in silence. Finally, Calypso spoke. In a strange language, with a lilting cadence. Will didn't understand the words, but Calypso pointed to the shore, where Gretchen lay.

Asia shook her head. "No."

Calypso laughed. So did the other seekriegers. She looked over at Will, and her eyes narrowed.

Behind him, Gretchen stirred. "Stay down," Will hissed.

"Where—" Gretchen looked around. Her eyes lit on the creatures in the bay.

"Don't move."

Calypso lashed out, slicing Asia across the face. Blood poured down her cheek—it was a cut identical to the one Will wore.

Gretchen screamed.

Calypso lunged for Asia, and the other seekriegers raced toward the shore.

"Run!" Will cried, urging Gretchen to her feet.

One of the seekriegers reached the edge of the bay, and Guernsey leaped up to meet her. The old Labrador sank her teeth into the seekrieger's leg. The siren let out a scream, but as Guernsey leaped at her throat, the seekrieger knocked her to the ground. Guernsey lay perfectly still, blood flowing from her crushed skull.

Will and Gretchen ran, but the seekriegers were too fast. They hadn't even reached the fields when one grabbed Will and dragged him by the legs toward the water.

"Gretchen!" Will screamed as he clawed at the sand, kicking at the seekrieger. It was worse than useless—her strength outmatched his a hundredfold.

"Will!" Gretchen shrieked as another seekrieger reached her and dragged her near the bay. Gretchen's screams reached a fevered pitch. The seekrieger wrapped an arm around her neck. But Gretchen pulled free of the seekrieger. Turning, she delivered a punch to the stomach that knocked the creature backward ten feet.

The seekrieger stumbled for a moment, then

leaped at Gretchen. But Gretchen twisted, throwing her to the ground. And when she turned to face Will, he barely recognized her. Her blue eyes burned red—completely red, with no whites. As Gretchen stalked toward them, the seekrieger holding Will shrieked, released her grip, and raced back into the water.

"Calypso!" Gretchen shouted in a voice that was not her own. It was deep and booming—like thunder. She strode into the water.

Calypso released her hold on Asia and smiled a snarling grin at Gretchen. She said something in her strange language.

"You're too late, Calypso," the Gretchen-creature said.

Asia's face registered terror. "The Fury has awoken," she said, and closed her eyes.

The seekriegers screeched and wailed. The water churned as they plunged below the surface. Gretchen strode into the water.

"No!" Will shouted. "Don't go to them!" He reached for Gretchen, but she grabbed his hand in a searing grip. He cried out in pain. She blinked with those strange red eyes, the color of blood, and seemed to recognize him.

Gretchen released him. "Get out of the water," she told him.

Will stumbled back as she spread her arms and plunged them into the sea. Fire spread from her hands, racing across the surface of the bay.

The seekriegers' screams rose like steam, sounding an alarm across the bay. Will clapped his hands over his ears and sank to his knees. The screams were like knives or a bed of nails pressing against him, slicing through his skin, peeling it back. . . .

Will stared at Gretchen—the Burning One, Asia had called her. Suddenly he realized what must have happened the night the seekriegers came for Tim. Gretchen had been there. She must have been. Somehow she fought them off and set the sail on fire to frighten them away. Then she dragged Will to shore. . . .

The seekriegers thrashed wildly, their figures dark against the fire. As it touched them, the flames turned purple, then red, and still the screams went on.

Slowly, slowly, they died away.

The red flames returned to yellow and orange. They burned on across the surface of the dark water as Will stood watching. He stood until he heard someone shouting his name and the faraway wail of police sirens.

Will stood watching, but the waters of the bay remained still.

Gretchen turned to face him. Her eyes were back to normal. She took a step toward him. Then another.

Then she fainted, dropping into the bay with a pale splash.

Gretchen's eyes fluttered open. "Will?"

"Hey," he said quietly, leaning forward in his chair. "You're back with us."

"Where—"

"Walfang General," Will told her.

Gretchen looked around the light beige room. "Is that why the wallpaper's so tasteful?"

"Pretty much."

She struggled to sit up, then instantly regretted it. Her muscles screamed, and she sat back against her pillow. "Take it easy," Will suggested.

"Could you have told me that ninety seconds ago?" Gretchen shot back.

"Aren't you supposed to be making a speech about how grateful you are to be alive?"

Gretchen sighed. "I am grateful." Something warm brushed her hand. Will's fingers had intertwined with hers. The beeping heart monitor speeded up, broadcasting her feelings across the room. She felt her face flush. Will was watching the monitor as if a new idea was just dawning on him.

"Oh, great, you're awake!" Angus said from the hallway. "Now you can make a statement for the paper."

Angus was right behind Gretchen's father, who had stopped short in the doorway, his dark eyes wide with relief. He had a white paper coffee cup in each hand.

"Hi, Dad," she said.

"Hi." Johnny fumbled with the coffee a moment, and handed a cup to Will. Then he set the other one down on the table beside Gretchen's bed and leaned over her. He touched her hair gently, then gave her a tender kiss on the forehead. Gretchen felt the familiar stubble on his cheek brush against her temple. "Hi," he said again. He looked at her with bright dark eyes, and she realized that he'd lost the faraway look he'd been wearing for days. It was as if they had both broken out of a dream.

"I'm okay," Gretchen told him.

He looked at her, his eyes filling with tears. "Good," he said.

As a speech, it lacked eloquence, but the way the tense, haggard lines of his face had softened said everything.

Angus flopped into the chair on the other side of Gretchen's bed. "So are you going to be my big story, or what?"

"Forget it, Angus. I don't even remember what happened." Gretchen sneaked a look at Will, who nodded.

"Is this friendship?" Angus demanded.

"What are you even doing here?" Gretchen asked.

"Angus called 911," Will told her. "He was the first one on the scene."

Gretchen looked at Angus, who shrugged. "Police scanner. Someone called in about some smoke."

"It was a pretty bad fire on the bay." Johnny took Gretchen's hand. "It's lucky Will pulled you from the water."

"Dude, that place is torched," Angus said. "They're closing the surrounding beaches until everything can get cleaned up."

"The town isn't happy," Will explained. "But it's almost the end of the season, so it could be worse."

"I'll say. Now maybe those shark things will move

on." Angus shook his head and took a swig from Will's coffee. "Ugh. Dude, don't you use sugar? This is vile."

"Sharks?" Johnny asked, his face a blend of confusion and amusement.

"Angus is convinced the waters are swimming with them," Will said quickly. "And that the town is hiding it." He tried to make the idea sound ridiculous, but Johnny didn't laugh.

"There are a lot of stories," Gretchen's dad said. "If you live out here long enough, you hear a few." He looked down at Gretchen, and everyone was silent for a while.

Gretchen let out an involuntary yawn.

"I'm sorry, sweetie," Johnny said. "We should let you rest."

"I'm not tired," Gretchen said.

"Right. Okay, well, how about if you just close your eyes and meditate a while? Or just read," Johnny suggested.

"I brought you the paper." Angus pointed to it on the bedside table.

"I'll go talk to the doctor about when you can get out of here." Johnny flashed Angus and Will a *let's go* look before starting toward the door.

"Will?" Gretchen called. "Hang on a minute, would you?"

"I'll catch up with you guys," Will told Johnny and Angus.

Gretchen scooted over, and he sat on the edge of her bed. Her eyes darted to the clock on the far wall.

"It's late," Gretchen observed.

Will nodded. "So late it's early."

"Your mom will be freaking out."

"I called my dad. I had to tell him about Guernsey. . . ."

The memory of the valiant dog flashed across Gretchen's mind. "Poor Guernsey." She covered Will's hand with her own.

Will's chin quivered. "She was a brave old girl."

"Yeah."

Will cleared his throat. "Dad is taking care of burying her. He said he'd calm Mom down, too. But she'll probably be here first thing in the morning with a basket of scones, so don't eat any of the hospital food."

"Your parents are so sweet," Gretchen said.

"You think so?" Will looked surprised.

"Yeah . . . don't you?" Gretchen cocked her head. "I mean, they're always trying to take care of you. Your mom freaks out every time you leave the house because she's so afraid. And your dad slaves away at that farm because he wants you to go to whatever college you want."

"He slaves away because he loves money."

"Money? Are you serious? If he wanted money, he could sell that farm and retire a millionaire."

"I guess they can but . . ." Will looked thoughtful. "I don't think of them that way."

They sat together in silence for a long moment.

Gretchen drew in a deep sigh, steeling herself to ask the question that hung over her like a dagger. "Is Asia . . ." The words hung in the air.

"Gone," Will told her.

"I'm sorry."

Will nodded, thinking. "I think she's probably . . . relieved." But Gretchen saw the tears burning in his eyes. "They're all gone, I think. Even Kirk should stop hearing them now."

"What happened?" Gretchen asked.

Will looked at her carefully. "You don't remember?"

She shook her head. "I remember those . . . things . . . and I remember Asia was there. But after that . . ."

Will's face was unreadable. "There was—" He took a long moment before speaking, as if weighing his words carefully. "There was a gas spill on the bay. The gas—ignited."

"How?"

Will bit his lip, hesitating. "Must have been a live cable or something."

Gretchen looked down at the pale blue blanket that was pulled up to her waist. "Will," she said at last, "there's something I have to tell you." She looked up into his eyes. "Will, I was there the night Tim died." The truth poured from her like pus from a wound. She cringed at what he would say.

Will put his hands to his face. He sighed deeply, then ran his hands through his hair. "I know," he said at last.

"You . . . know?" Gretchen repeated. "How?"

"It just—you had to be, right? Someone dragged me from the water to the beach. Who else would have?"

Gretchen touched her forehead. "I don't remember it."

"Do you know why you rescued me?" Will asked. "Why me, and not Tim?"

Gretchen felt this question like a stab to the heart. "Because I . . ." She swallowed, trying to make sound come from her lips.

Will watched her. She knew how badly he needed an answer. But in the end she couldn't say it—she couldn't tell him that she would always have chosen Will over his brother. "I don't know," she said at last. "Maybe it was too late for him."

Will nodded. "Asia told me that the seekriegers were drawn to people who were angry, or sad, or feeling something dark, you know. So why did they take Tim?" Gretchen remembered the conversation she'd had with Tim just hours before he disappeared. Tim had told her that he loved her. She'd told Tim that she loved Will. *Was his heart so broken that the seekriegers felt drawn to it?* It hurt her to think that she had caused him so much pain.

"I'm sorry," Gretchen whispered.

"You can't save everyone, Gretchen," he told her.

Tears rolled down her cheeks, silent as a secret.

"Stop. It's okay." Will put a finger to her lips. "Gretchen . . ." He held her hands in his large warm ones. "Can I just tell you something? I'm just so glad that you're here."

"You are?"

"It's hard enough without Tim. I don't know what I would've done if you . . ." He shook his head, unable to say more.

Gretchen looked away, pretending to inspect the

pretty wallpaper. She thought about spending the next year in Walfang. Maybe that was what she and Will both needed. *Perhaps the only way out is through,* Gretchen thought. *I can't leave until we've put the past behind us.*

Will leaned forward and placed a warm kiss on her forehead.

"What's that for?"

Will smiled. "For you."

Gretchen's heart fluttered as she settled back against the cool pillow. It was the kiss of a friend, of someone close to a brother. She still loved him beyond that, but she knew Will wasn't ready for anything more right now. They both had some healing to do.

But, for the first time, it seemed as if that might actually be possible.

As Angus said, the sharks had moved on.

Author's Note

The allusions to the *Odyssey* are correct, although the action that takes place after the epic is my own invention, as is the word *seekrieger*. It's a combination of two German words that, literally translated, mean "sea warrior," which is how I thought of Calypso's band of sirens. The town of Walfang is loosely based on Bridgehampton, New York, where my family has a house and where I have spent every summer since I was fourteen. Although there are many traditional sea chanteys about mermaids, those that appear in this book are my original work. The captain's log that appears here is intended as an homage to Bram Stoker's *Dracula*, in which a similarly terrifying captain's log makes an appearance.

Don't miss

Fury's Fire,

the sequel to

Siren's Storm

Coming Summer 2012 from

Alfred A. Knopf Books for Young Readers

Published by Alfred A. Knopf, an imprint of
Random House Children's Books

Ice begets ice and flame begets flame;
Those that go down never rise up again.
—Sailors' proverb

An uneasy weight hung on Gretchen's chest as she looked around the dim room. *I was dreaming something—what was it?* Gretchen's mind cast about for a train of thought, but clutched at emptiness. She couldn't remember. She knew only that she was glad to be awake.

It was that moment before sunrise when the sky has begun to turn gray and the world is filled with shadows. The room was still, but the yellow curtains near her bureau fluttered slightly, and fear skittered down her spine with quick spider steps.

"Who's there?" Gretchen asked.

There was a sound like a sigh, and Gretchen's chest constricted in fear. Something was there. By the window. A dark presence. She could almost make out the shape of a man behind the yellow cloth.

Her voice tightened in her throat; she couldn't scream. Someone was in her room. Gretchen's mind reeled about—it was Kirk. Crazy Kirk—the sophomore who babbled incoherently about seekriegers and angels—had come to kill her. He had stolen into her room before, to give her a painting, a coded message that only he could decipher. . . .

"Kirk?" she whispered. Her voice sounded loud in the still and silent room.

Gretchen sat up. "Kirk?" she said again. She blinked, and the light shifted. The dim gray lifted, like fog burning away in the sun. Suddenly everything looked different, and she could see clearly.

There was nothing there.

The curtains sagged, and Gretchen understood her mistake. The folds fell at odd angles, suggesting a human form. But the presence she had sensed earlier had disappeared completely.

"Dream cobwebs," Gretchen said aloud. That was what her father, Johnny Ellis, called it when you woke up and still had traces of your nightmares clinging to your mind. She pushed back her covers and swung her legs over the side of her bed, and something tore at her ankle.

Gretchen screamed, jumping backward as her cat, Bananas, tumbled from beneath her bed skirt. The feline rolled onto her back playfully, then sat up and curled her tail around her feet, as if nothing had happened and she had no idea why Gretchen was acting so dramatic.

"Cat—" Gretchen started.

Bananas just looked at her, then nonchalantly began to groom her paw.

"Licking my flesh from your claws?" Gretchen

asked, rubbing the scratch on her foot. It wasn't bad, really, but it did itch. As if she was offended by the question, the orange-and-white-striped cat turned and strutted out the half-open door.

As the striped tail disappeared, Gretchen cast another glance toward the window. *It was just a dream,* she told herself.

The light shone through the curtains now, and she could see the shape of the tree beyond the window. There was nothing left of the dark presence . . . nothing but the feeling of dread that still sat in Gretchen's chest.

Gretchen yanked off her nightgown and pulled on a pair of red running shorts. She tugged on her sports bra and then ducked into an ancient T-shirt advertising the Old Mill, a cafe in one of the neighboring towns. When she lived in Manhattan, Gretchen used to run along the reservoir in Central Park. It was near her Upper East Side apartment, and Gretchen liked being near the water . . . and the fact that the water was surrounded by an enormous chain-link fence. She could see it, but she couldn't fall in. Gretchen thought water was beautiful—but it frightened her.

Gretchen never ran much at the summerhouse. There were no sidewalks along the street by the house, so it wasn't really convenient. But now that she and her father were going to be living here full-time, she was going to have to find a way. Running was what kept her head clear in the cold months. And even though it was only the end of September, the mornings were already turning chilly.

"What are you doing here?" Gretchen asked as she tramped into the kitchen. Her father was sitting at the Formica table, sipping from a cup of coffee and halfheartedly skimming the *New York Times*.

"I live here, remember?" Johnny said. He smiled at her, but it was a smile like a heavy weight—as if it were taking all of his facial muscles an effort to make it happen.

"Don't pretend like you're some kind of early riser." Gretchen reached for a banana. "It's six-thirty."

"Couldn't sleep."

Gretchen frowned. "That's not good."

Johnny shrugged. "It happens." He took another long pull of coffee. "I'll feel better once everything arrives."

He meant the things from their Manhattan apartment. Once Johnny had given up the lease, it had taken only two hours for the building manager to find a new tenant. They had been replaced in true New York City style—immediately and without mercy.
"When do the movers get here?" Gretchen asked.

"Tomorrow."

Gretchen nodded. She would feel better once she had her things from the apartment, too. Even though she would miss living in Manhattan, she was ready to close that chapter of her life, to write The End above it instead of having the pages go on and on with no clear purpose. *Besides,* she thought, *we need the money.*

When her mother moved out, she had kept custody of most of the funds. Yvonne was an heiress and knew about investments; Johnny had never been in charge of the finances before. So, for a few years, things went on exactly as they had before. Manhattan private school, expensive rent for the apartment, trips abroad. Then, quite suddenly, Johnny realized that they were out of money. A few bad investments and several years of living beyond their means had left them in terrible debt. So they were abandoning the apartment and living in what Gretchen liked to think of as "the ancestral home"—the old farmhouse her grandfather had bought over half a century ago, which Johnny had inherited, and which he owned free and clear.

As if he were reading her thoughts about finances, Johnny leaned onto one hip and reached for his wallet. "Listen, I wanted to give you something so you could do some back-to-school shopping—" He riffled through the bills, which were mostly ones, and pulled out two twenties. Wincing, he held them out. "I know it's not much."

Gretchen didn't reach for the cash. "It's okay, Dad. I have a job, remember?"

"You're not keeping that job, are you?"

"Sure. Why not?"

Johnny touched the lotus tattoo on his temple. "It's your senior year, Gretchie. You need to keep your grades up."

"They'll stay up."

"That's the most important thing."

"I know, Dad. But I'm going to have to have a job while I'm in college, right? I might as well get used to it."

Johnny looked like he'd been slapped. "I guess I—"

"I didn't—I didn't mean that in a bad way." Gretchen stumbled over her words. "I just meant—"

Johnny dropped the bills on the table. "No, you're right." He shook his head. "I'm sorry, Gretchen."

She touched his shoulder. "It's okay, Dad."

He put his hand over hers, but did not look at her. She gave him a playful poke on the shoulder, but he just sighed. "I never worried about money," he admitted. "I guess I thought musicians weren't supposed to care about it."

Gretchen nodded, but she felt her thoughts clouding. The truth—if she dared tell it to herself—was that she was furious with her father for losing all their money. For not caring enough. For not taking care of things. She didn't want to live on Long Island for her senior year. She didn't want to switch schools. She didn't want to stay near the bay, near the bad memories. . . .

But she also loved Johnny. And one of the things that she loved about him was that he didn't care about money and things in the way that her mother did. Johnny loved people and he loved experiences. He didn't care about cars or jewelry or the right crowd.

She gave him a quick kiss on his tattoo. "Love you."

He looked up at her with his deep gray eyes. "I love you, too, Sugar Bunny."

Gretchen laughed and tossed the banana peel into the trash. She waved over her shoulder as she headed out the door, her sneakers crunching the gravel still wet with dew.

Gretchen loped along the patchy grass by the side

of the road, starting with an easy trot. She passed the falling-down old potato barn, gray in the mist, that marked the point at which the Ellis land ended and the Archer farm began. Her muscles were tight, but each pace warmed her, loosening them. A light breeze swept the clammy air over her skin.

She heard a clatter and rumble behind her. Trucks often used this route as a cut-through to the highway. Gretchen moved to the right slightly and kept running. The engine hummed, picking up speed, and the tires crunched over the asphalt as the truck bore down on her.

Gretchen screeched and slammed her shoulder into a hedgerow as the black truck sped past, spewing dirt and rocks with its oversized tires. A chunk of gravel nicked Gretchen's calf. She cursed and inspected the scratch. She would probably have a bruise later, but it wasn't bad. Her heart hammered in her chest as she looked after the truck, which had already disappeared into the mist. She had thought of getting the license plate thirty seconds too late.

What would I have done, anyway? she wondered. *Called the police? The driver probably just didn't see me in the mist.*

Her legs felt weak as she crossed the street. For a moment, she considered going back home. But she didn't want to. Momentum carried her forward, and she gathered speed as she ran across the Archer property. She passed the flowering squash patch, the heavy yellow flowers bowing under the weight of the gathered mist. Here and there, pale orange butternut or fat red kuri squashes peeked out from wide green leaves. The squash patch was a long, slim strip—most of the summer people were gone by the end of September, and there wasn't much of a market for winter squash. Still, some people bought the ornamental gourds and pumpkins. And there were enough gourmet cooks and local restaurants to make the delicatas and carnival squashes worth the ground they grew in.

Gretchen ran past dormant fields and into the small copse of trees. There was little mist here, although it was dark with shade. Still, Gretchen navigated easily. The Archer land was as familiar to her as her own, given that her two best childhood friends, Will and Tim, had grown up here.

Through the trees and out toward the sand. The muscles in Gretchen's legs strained with the change in terrain as she ran along the mix of sand and rock. Mist hung over the water in a cottony blanket, and a single dark rock jutted up through the layer of fog like a grasping arm. The early-morning sun struggled to break through the clouds, managing only to send down a few pale bars that disappeared before reaching the earth.

Gretchen ran farther, then stopped to rest on a rock. It had been months since she had run, and—although her body felt good—she wasn't used to it. Part of the mist had burned off, and she could see the dark green water, smooth as glass. There was no evidence of the minnows and crabs that lived in that water, and Gretchen imagined them still sleeping, dreaming their watery dreams.

She pulled at her shirt, which clung to her body with a mix of sweat and fog, and picked up a small stone. It was gray, with a white line across the center, smooth and oval. Tim had taught her how to skip a rock across the water ages ago, and she held it between thumb and forefinger and skimmed it out over the water. It bounced once, twice, three times, then hurled itself forward for the final fourth bounce and landed with a plop.

"Tim could do seven," Gretchen murmured, leaning back on her elbows. She pictured handsome, ten-year-old Tim, grinning as his rock danced over the water. Poor Will. He could only send a rock bursting into the water like a cannonball.

Gretchen watched the rings spreading from the point of final impact. *Pretty*, she thought, watching the fog roll back like a slow wave. A pale disk appeared at the place where her rock had pierced the water. She cocked her head, watching. A ring formed around the edge of the disk and didn't disappear. Instead, it grew darker.

Like an eye, Gretchen thought. Her body felt cold suddenly, and she was aware of her damp shirt clinging to her skin.

Mist swirled around the dark ring, twisting upward, spouting an oval wall. It gained volume and grew, like a pillar, toward the dark cloud above. The cyclone writhed, snakelike, and slithered slowly toward her.

Gretchen leaned backward slightly, but felt hypnotized by the waterspout. It moved slowly at first, then more quickly. Gretchen struggled to her feet. She stumbled backward and fell, the rock tearing into her flesh right where the gravel spewed by the truck had hit her. Her hair blew around her face as the wind shrieked like a screaming ghoul.

The waterspout reached toward her, and for a moment Gretchen thought she saw a woman's face—hideous and terrible—in the writhing core. Air blasted her hair like a wild, cold breath of some ferocious, devouring animal. She screamed and tried to struggle away as the waterspout moved toward her. But as it reached the edge of the water, it dissipated into the air as suddenly as it had appeared.

Gretchen froze, staring in disbelief. She was so focused on the emptiness before her that she shrieked as a hand clutched her arm.

"Easy," said a voice.

Gretchen looked up into the face of Bertrand Archer—Will's dad. His brow was wrinkled with concern as his warm brown eyes looked down at her. "They can't do much once they reach the land."

"You saw it?" That was a relief. At least she hadn't been hallucinating.

"Waterspouts—not that uncommon around here. Seen 'em a few times."

Mr. Archer let go of her hand, and she realized she was shaking. So did he, apparently, because he caught hold of her hand again. For a moment, he said nothing. Just looked at her. "Strange weather."

Gretchen nodded.

"Maybe it's not a good idea to be out by the water like this. Tell you what—why don't you come on home with me? I'm sure Evelyn's cooked up something for breakfast."

The thought of the Archers' warm yellow kitchen calmed her. "Yes, thank you."

Mr. Archer gave a curt nod, and turned. Gretchen followed him.

But she couldn't help casting a final glance over her shoulder.

The surface of the water was smooth as glass again, hiding the dreams and intent of the creatures that lay beneath.